THUG LIFE 3

Trai'Quan

Lock Down Publications and Ca$h Presents

Thug Life 3

A Novel by *Trai'Quan*

Trai'Quan

Lock Down Publications
P.O. Box 944
Stockbridge, Ga 30281

Copyright 2021 by Trai'Quan
Thug Life 3

All rights reserved. No part of this book may be reproduced in any form or by electronic or mechanical means, including information storage and retrieval systems without permission in writing from the publisher, except by a reviewer who may quote brief passages in review.
First Edition April 2021
Printed in the United States of America

This is a work of fiction. Names, characters, places, and incidents either are products of the author's imagination or are used fictitiously. Any similarity to actual events or locales or persons, living or dead, is entirely coincidental.

Lock Down Publications
Like our page on Facebook: Lock Down Publications @
www.facebook.com/lockdownpublications.ldp
Cover design and layout by: **Dynasty Cover Me**
Book interior design by: **Shawn Walker**
Edited by: **Lashonda Johnson**

4

Stay Connected with Us!

Text **LOCKDOWN** to 22828 to stay up-to-date with new releases, sneak peaks, contests and more…

Thank you!

Submission Guideline.

Submit the first three chapters of your completed manuscript to ldpsubmissions@gmail.com, subject line: Your book's title. The manuscript must be in a .doc file and sent as an attachment. Document should be in Times New Roman, double spaced and in size 12 font. Also, provide your synopsis and full contact information. If sending multiple submissions, they must each be in a separate email.

Have a story but no way to send it electronically? You can still submit to LDP/Ca$h Presents. Send in the first three chapters, written or typed, of your completed manuscript to:

LDP: Submissions Dept
P.O. Box 944
Stockbridge, Ga 30281

DO NOT send original manuscript. Must be a duplicate.

Provide your synopsis and a cover letter containing your full contact information.
Thanks for considering LDP and Ca$h Presents.

Acknowledgements

This book is especially dedicated to my sister, Tiffany, my cousin, Monica, and my cousin, Lisa. All three have been there for me when no one else was there. They are 3 lionesses inside of a large jungle, always looking out for their Pride. To me, family means everything.

To my home, my heart, Augusta, Ga. The city tore down my neighborhood (Sunset). But no one can destroy the love everyone in my neighborhood had.

My mother, Charlsie Simpkins, who passed away in 2006.

To all of the people who support me and purchase my books. I love you people. And without you, I would be nobody. To Cash, much love Sun, the Queen Shawn for her work on my books, and everyone at Lockdown Publications, who I don't know, I appreciate you.

Trai'Quan

Prologue

Last days of Spring 1999

The Sun was unusually hot, beaming down and spreading its warmth to all of the fresh flowers and plant life. School was about to be out soon, and all of the kids would be preparing to enjoy the summer. But it wasn't quite summer yet. And it was still hot outside. In fact, it was about to get even hotter outside.

"Alright, Nassa, that's their Blazer right there," Trish Blaylock said to her youngest daughter, as she eased the 1998 Suburban up behind the smoke grey Blazer. Vanessa was only ten years old, but tall for a girl of her age. Sitting behind the wheel of the large SUV, she looked like a teenager. She had a deadly serious look upon her face, as she gripped the steering wheel like she meant business.

"These muthafuckaz don't know who they playing wit," Trish cursed, as she slid the clip into the black on black AK-47. Then she pulled the latch back. "But they about to muthafuckin find out," she added, turning half way around in the passenger seat to look into the back seat at her other two daughters.

"You bitches ready? Y'all ain't scared, are you?" she asked.

Sixteen-year-old Diane looked up with an intense look in her eyes. She slid the hold of the Mack II back. "I ain't scared of shit," she stated. "You must be talking to Brina."

"Nah, un," Brina announced, pushing the clip into the Uzi 9mm that she held in her twelve-year-old hands. "I ain't scared of shit, either."

Both of them were taking full advantage of their opportunity to curse without being popped in the mouth, which wasn't that often.

"Alright. Then let's take care of these muthafuckaz. I've got shit to do."

***

The smoked out GMC Blazer came to a stop behind a school bus. Because there was a red light at the time, there was no reason for the driver of the Blazer to blow his horn. After all, it was a bus filled with children.

"Put sum fiya on the oter blunt, Mon, and pass the bitch," one of the island boys in the back seat called out.

"Yez, Mon. Me already mad. Me didn't get to kill nobody yet."

There were five of them in the Blazer. Having come to Augusta right after their cousin TJ had been killed, they'd come because someone had speculated that TJ had been robbed. The police didn't mention anything about the cocaine that TJ had just brought back to Augusta, and they knew he had it. The question was what happened to it.

"I'm telling you, mon," he said as he inhaled deeply, "Dat bitch got da dope," one of them said, and then coughed.

"You tink so?" The driver asked. Then he thought about it for a moment. "I just don't tink the bitch killed 'im," he stated.

"Boy, ya stupid. We got many bitches dat'll blow a niggaz 'eart out 'im chest," another one said.

That's true, the driver thought. He was just about to verbally agree when something caught his attention. He looked into the side mirror and could have sworn that he saw a woman walking in the street, a beautiful black woman, and she had her left arm behind her back.

"Yo, mon. You see dis bitch?" He asked.

Just when it seemed that everyone was shaking their high and turning to look, they all seemed to see her and the two other girls at the same time. Then they saw the guns. "Oh shit, mon. Pull off. Pull off," one of them shouted. But it was too late.

***

Trish braced the AK-47 between her shoulder and her neck. She saw the driver's eyes open wide when he saw her bring the gun up. It seemed that time stood still and everything became quiet as her finger squeezed the trigger.
Thrrr. Attt. Thrrr. Attt. Thrrr. Attt.
The AK-47 began to spit like it wanted everybody to hear its voice. On the other side of the SUV, Diane swung the Mack II from side to side, spraying the entire passenger side of the Blazer while Sabrina and her Uzi sprayed the back.

All three of them burned off one full extended clip each, and then there was silence.

"Alright," Trish said loud enough for them to hear her, "Let's get the fuck outta here before the cops come."

As they turned to leave, Diane happened to glance up at the bus. She wasn't surprised to see all of the kids on it had their faces plastered against the window, but there was one face that stood out. A boy that was the same age as her, and just happened to be in her 3rd period class at school. She looked directly into his eyes and saw him smile as she began to turn.

***

When you visit the zoo, don't get it confused. Those animals are domesticated and/or complacent within their current

11

reality, having accepted their reality. They realize they are *not* re-entering the wild. The zoo is their home now.

But in the Jungle, those rules didn't apply. In the jungle, there was nothing sweet. The animals had to hunt in order to eat. Survival was the number one rule. And only the strong would end up surviving the wild, because in the Jungle, the animals made the rules.

This is another Trai Quan Original.

Chapter One
A Call of the Wild

Present Day

"What the fuck you mean you ain't got my money?" Diane held the cell phone away from her face and looked at it like it had just turned into a viper. Upon realizing that it hadn't, she brought it back to her ear and listened.

"Nah, D, let me explain," the caller on the other end cried out to her.

She sighed.

"Shit just ain't going right for me. Niggaz ran up into one of my spots and robbed some niggaz who get they work from me. That shit fucked me up. And if that wasn't enough, cops ran down on my niggaz out in Farrington. A nigga took a major loss out there."

He paused in his speech, as if he had to catch his breath, and Diane waited.

"Look, D. A nigga ain't trying yo gangsta. I can get them stacks back to you. But a nigga gone take a serious loss to do it," he stated.

"Okay. So what do you want me to do?" she asked.

At the moment, she was sitting inside of the unisex hair and nail salon called "Flashy." There was one girl doing her weave and another doing her nails. The girl that was doing her nails glanced up at her when she heard the tone of her voice. Everybody knew who D'Block was. In the streets, her name was damn near synonymous to Michael Myers and Jason, except she wore stiletto heels and carried a .44 like it was her second lover. The Glock 17 was her first.

But she didn't want to fall out with this nigga for two reasons. First, the nigga spent too much money with her. In fact, he was one of her top five best buyers. The nigga was getting three to five bricks every trip. Secondly, since Young Castro had placed her in this type of position, she had to admit, other than her two sisters, Brina and Nessa, only Maine, Big Steve, Izzy, and Man-Man were really buying big. Young said that all of his Lieutenants needed to be moving birds. He had too much product coming in and needed to move it as fast as possible.

"A'ight, nigga. It's a good thing I'm in a good mood right now," she said into the phone.

Her good mood, and the fact that Young didn't want her out in the streets killing anybody, had just saved him.

"I'ma give you some more time. I don't need none of you niggaz to go out of business. So I'ma hit you wit another Pine Apple. Nigga, don't fuck that shit up," she warned.

"I won't, D. I promise," And 1 said.

"Don't promise, nigga. Hustle. And yo, you gone owe a bitch double, too. But I'ma give you time to pay it. Ya heard?" she asked.

"I got you, baby. And I'ma get that to you, too." He ended the call.

Diane slid the phone back into her jeans pocket. Then she sat there thinking while she was getting her hair and nails done.

***

"The fuck you mean we're sharing power wit' a bitch, nigga?" T-Roy looked over at his twin.

Troy and Leroy Worthy were the most notorious drug kingpins from the Sand Hills area, extending all the way to Martinez-Evans. The only reason they'd never extended down into the heart of Augusta was because the money on the Hill was better. The only thing that was competing with it was over across the bridge. They'd been doing their thing since 2010, and earned their respect the hard way. Since they'd moved to Augusta, shit was hot in the city. And them having just left the 'A' because their names were ringing too loud, they hadn't wanted to get themselves hot like that. So they chose to put it down up on the Hill.

From 2010 until the end of 2011, everything was good. They were getting major money. Their only real competition had been Juggernaut and the Jamaican nigga, Mishna. But then Juggernaut got killed, and Mishna was in prison for manslaughter. After that, shit seemed to have fluctuated. And then this young nigga Young Castro got his weight up. Troy thought for sure that they were headed into a war with Young Castro and his team, but some other motherfuckers got in their way, and Young Castro seemed to have taken a step back. Then this bitch Diane Blaylock, AKA D-Block, seemed to have stepped out of a fucking comic book.

"Listen, Shawty," Leroy spoke. "The bitch ain't really that much of an issue, Shawty. She got what she got going on down there, and we up here, Shawty."

"That bitch better stay down there, too, Shawty. Fuck around and I'll wake these dogs up." He was referring to the Bloods, and 75% of the Hill were homies, so they weren't really worried about anyone coming into their spot. Besides that, they both had some major stain.

"Don't even worry about it, Shawty," Leroy told him. "So what's up? We gon' hit the club tonight, or what, Shawty?"

Club Cloud 9 was the hot spot now, especially with Fusion going out of business. Fusion had been a club across the bridge in Beech Island S.C. and, for a while, they'd been the hottest spot. But Club 360 out on Gordon Hwy had them a nice run for the money. All of that was then. Right now, it was all about

Cloud 9. Well, it was until this new club on Mike Padgett Hwy opened. That one was being called Magic City.

"Yeah, Shawty," T-Roy said. "I still say we should open our own club, Shawty. We could get all of these country niggaz money, Shawty."

"I know, Shawty. But we trying to keep a low profile, too," Leroy stated. "Shawty, we don't need that shit from the 'A' following us down here."

They'd made a fast getaway from Atlanta because of a drug war they'd been involved in, which wasn't even their war. Some of their GF homies were going toe to toe with a few of the gangs. They were both related to one of the Good Fellas, Capo. And now their names were in the police's ears about a triple homicide.

"Yeah, you right, Shawty," T-Roy sulked.

But he knew there was no way around what his twin had just pointed out to him. They didn't need the extra attention.

***

"Why my nigga fucks wit' this high yellow bitch, I don't even know," Diane spoke the words to herself. But even as she did, both the girl doing her nails and the one doing her hair looked up.

They all watched as Imani and her girl, Nico, stepped inside. Imani was the one Diane was talking about. Wearing her Fendi blouse, Seven jeans, and Giuseppe heels, while holding the expensive Gucci bag, and *too* much jewelry, Imani was younger than her, at only 29. At one point, all of her 5'10" frame had been like a model. Back then, she'd been thin, almost white girl slim. That was until Maine had put a baby in her. Now she had a body, with a small waist line, nice hips, and an ass. She wasn't thin any more, she was thick.

"What's up, bitches?" Imani spoke with a wide smile and too much lip gloss on. "Reese, gurl, are we too early for hair appointments?"

There were six chairs inside of the place. And at the moment, all six of them were full. But the heavy set, dark skin woman, who was doing hair at the back chair, looked up and slightly rolled her eyes.

"Bitch," she stated. "You know damn well y'all early. Your appointment ain't until 2:00. It's only 1:30. But you know I got you, gurl."

"That's what's up," Imani said, acting all white girly.

Diane watched as the two light skin women moved to take seats on the lounge sofa. Neither one of them even glanced her way. But even as she saw Imani pull her iPhone out, she had the feeling the bitch was aware of her. She just wasn't letting on that she was.

She couldn't tell Main to fire the bitch because he had a son by her stupid ass. And even if he didn't, Diane knew he wouldn't listen. The nigga was damn near bat shit crazy and had a thing for light skin bitches.

She shifted her focus. Diane was trying to figure out what exactly Big Dredd wanted her to do with his niece. Today was Tuesday, and from what he'd explain to her on the phone, this girl, Alicia, would be in Augusta sometime Friday. She was coming from Florida. And from what Noel told her, the girl was going through some things down there and he wanted to get her away from whatever was going on down there. But Diane didn't know what he expected her to do. Shit, with Young Castro making her the Senior Lieutenant and giving her so much product, she really didn't have time to do a lot of anything. Now he wanted her to look after the young girl. Please.

Trai'Quan

Chapter Two

Diane pulled the burgundy 2012 Denali into the driveway of her house, a two story 4 bedroom 2 ½ bath house that sat in a nice gated community in Hephzibah, GA. She parked right next to Damian's black 4.6 HSE Range Rover. She grabbed her Dolce & Gabbana bag and exited the SUV. Her Krakoff heels clacked up the driveway. Not seeing Justices' ESV Escalade, she didn't think he would be there. As soon as she opened the door and stepped inside, her three year old son, Nike, ran up to her.

"Mama."

She scooped him up as she closed the door and began to walk towards the den.

"How's mama's baby? Where Dada and your sister?" she asked.

Sure enough, he pointed in the direction she was walking. When she turned the corner and stepped through the doorway, she saw one year old Dawn asleep on the couch next to Damian, who seemed to be lost in his online Splinter Cell game. Diane sucked her teeth as she let Nike down.

"That's all you been doing all day?" she asked.

Damian glanced up.

"Oh, what's up, ma," he said. "Nah, I let your girl Breeze go early. She said there was something she had to do. But I ain't been here all day."

Breeze was her babysitter. The girl was pretty good for a sixteen year old, especially considering the amount of money Diane paid her to look after Nike and Dawn.

"Oh yeah?" She cocked her head as she placed her left hand upon her hip. "So what you been up to?" she asked, catching the way her baby's father glanced up.

"Ma, you know we don't get into each other's business like that," he responded. "You already know."

"Whatever, nigga." She turned and headed to their bedroom.

Once there, she tossed her bag on to the bed and then moved over to their walk-in closet. Diane kicked her heels off and began to remove her clothes. When she re-dressed, she pulled on jeans and a black long sleeve mesh shirt. She topped that off with a pair of all black Air Max. She then pulled on the double-breasted shoulder holsters. She slid her ladies edition .44 under her left arm, and the Glock .17 under her right arm. Then she slipped the S & W model 39 9mm into the back of her waist line. Once that was done, she pulled on her extended men's Brooks Brothers black trench coat. When she looked at her image in the full length mirror, she smiled.

"Mami gotta get that paper," she said.

***

The basketball game was held under the street lights. It was late in the evening and already dark. The only people out were the street walkers, dope boys, and junkies. The game was being played by the dope boys' workers, while the bosses stood on the sidelines, clutching hands full of money.

"Slow that shit down, nigga," Izzy called out to his team. At the moment, they had the ball.

The score was 34 to 40. They were behind by 6, and Izzy had five grand riding on it. But this nigga Burner was running his boys like they were fuckin' NBA draft picks or something. Izzy couldn't figure out where he got these niggaz from. Burner and his partner, Jersey, ran both Pepper Ridge and Quail Hollow. They were both originally from New Jersey, but had been in Augusta for the past year.

Izzy turned his head when he heard the loud music. There weren't too many people bumping Jadakiss like that, so he kinda knew it was D-Block before he saw the black on black Tahoe bend the corner. He knew she had her Denali, but he also knew that D-Block never drove it when there was the possibility that she would have to put in work. Thus, the Tahoe was her latest work vehicle. The truck turned into the parking lot, and pulled up right next to his Lexus GS, which he'd had fully custom designed.

"Damn," he cursed. "I wonder what the fuck I done did."

D-Block never really pulled up like that unless there was a problem. As he watched, Izzy saw her open the door and step out. When she turned and walked towards him, he sighed. She didn't have either one of her sisters with her, which meant that she might not be on the bullshit. Several people out there had their eyes on her, including Burner. All of them knew who she was and what she was about, so they were watching to see who was in trouble.

"What's up Izzy?" D-Block spoke as she came to a stop right next to him. Then she looked across the court and nodded her head to Burner.

"Uh, what's up, D?" Izzy stuttered.

"So, what's the score? Who's winning?" she asked.

"Uh. We're down by 4 now," he said.

They watched as the other team got possession and drove back down the court. They scored.

"Fuck," Izzy cursed.

From the corner of his eye, he could see that she looked down at the money in his hand.

"So, uh, D," Izzy began. "I know a nigga ain't fucked up nothing. Should I be worried? Then he turned his head and looked at her.

"Relax, baby. This ain't about you," D-Block stated.

21

Izzy followed the direction of her eyes. She was looking directly at Burner.

"What you know about the nigga Thug?" She asked. "He been making any noise out here?"

"Him and his people been keeping it in Pepper Ridge and Quail Hollow. They ain't bumpin' heads wit' nobody that I know of."

Silence. For a moment, neither of them spoke. Diane was going over the information she'd received. Word was, this nigga Burner, and his partner, Jersey, were getting their work from this New York nigga, who was plotting a takeover. Supposedly, they thought it was safe, since Young Castro fell back.

But she knew the truth. Young was getting too much cocaine to be having his name in the streets, so him, Jeeta, Poe and Cream all fell back and now ran their legal business. He still received the work, which was how the streets stayed flooded. Young had given her this position. He asked her to ease up, not to be too reckless in the streets, and not to murk anybody in broad daylight.

"These up north niggaz might become a problem," she said, still watching the game.

"I thought you and your sister's stepped out of the spotlight, unless it became necessary," he stated.

"See, that's what happens when niggaz think too hard." Diane smiled. "That's why I'm the Boss, and you're not. But just so you know," she turned and began to walk back towards her truck, but paused. "If it becomes necessary, then one of my teams gone come through. If that happens," she smiled. "Well, ya know how it can get out here in the Jungle." With that said, she walked off.

Izzy took a moment to watch the sway of her hips. Not too many people knew about the "Street Sweepers." The only reason Izzy even knew was because he'd had to drive for them once. The Street Sweepers were D-Block's baby's daddy, his mans Justice, a nigga from Apple Valley named Maine, and his partner, who was only known by Thugg. And neither one of them were to be fucked with. So yeah, if one of her teams came through, shit was gon' get hectic for a lot of muthafuckaz.

***

As soon as Burner saw the Tahoe pull out of the parking lot, he lost all focus of the game. The big homie Swole told them not to make any move against these niggaz until he gave the word, but he and Jersey were in Augusta by themselves. Swole was back home in Queens, N.Y. Burner had already investigated this bitch. He'd heard all of the rumors, the legends and fantasies, but he still hadn't seen any proof of this bitch being that tough, not in the last year. Her sister, Sabrina, had ties to these "LOE Life" niggaz. And the baby girl had just had a son for this nigga Cream. While Cream was an up top nigga himself, he'd just opened a Baskin Robbins. Neither he nor his crew were in the streets any longer, which meant they weren't a threat.

So this Bitch was actually the only Blaylock girl running shit. They could have already gotten her out of the way, but Swole said to hold up. They didn't know who she got her work from. And for her to be pushing the kind of weight they'd heard of, she had to be connected to some powerful people. Swole wanted to know who those people were, before they set shit into motion.

Then there was the Baby Daddy. That nigga might be the problem. Burner had heard a couple of rumors about that nigga and his partner. But when he sent word back home to his cousins in Brooklyn to ask if they knew these niggaz, all they said was most niggaz would cross the street instead of crossing them, but nobody gave details. *That's strange*, he thought.

Chapter Three

Diane was standing on the front porch when the royal blue Dodge Durango with the chrome and black Lexani rims pulled up into her driveway. The truck parked directly behind Damian's Escalade, and the door opened on the driver side. Diane took a sip of her pink champagne as she watched the younger woman exit the truck, wearing Fendi jeans that seem to be too tight on her thick hips, and a nice Valente blouse, along with a pair of Chelsea boots.

Well, Diane thought, *at least I don't have to teach her how to dress.*

She smiled at the young, dark skin woman, who was now walking towards her. Alicia wore her hair in dreadlocks that hung down to just below her shoulders. They held a reddish tint, and were blonde at the tips. She also had dimples in her cheeks, and what appeared to be blue contacts in her eyes. She came to a stop at the bottom of the steps and looked up at Diane.

"Yu de one mi spoke to on de phone?" she asked, speaking patois.

"Yeah. I'm the one your uncle asked to look after you. Where are your bags?" Diane asked.

"Dey in de truck," Alicia stated. "So mi be staying wit yu den."

"Yeah, for a while anyway," Diane told her. "Once you get used to the city, and if you decide you need some more space, then you can move out. But for now, I've got a guest bedroom for you."

For a moment, both women looked at one another in silence, sort of sizing one another up.

"Eard yu was di lioness in di jungle. Mi uncle, 'im say yu di real rude bitch."

"Heard the same thing about you." Diane smiled back at the younger woman. "But look, we can measure clit sizes later. Let's get you settled in.

***

His mother named him Pharaoh. That's the name she bestowed upon him when he was born, thirty years ago. But one juvenile trip and one brief prison visit when he was eighteen had people giving him the nickname Thugg. But that was mostly because of the way he handled himself in the streets.

Thugg wasn't a dope boy, he wasn't about to stand out on the corners and take those types of chances. He did his dirt in the streets, but he wasn't stupid. Nah, Thugg didn't get down like that. After his prison trip, he'd decided that he wasn't about to go back, and hoped that it never came down to it, especially about something as stupid as standing on a corner. Because, in his mind, if the cops came to get him for some serious shit, then he was going to hold court in the streets. Shit, if it started in the streets, it would end in them.

But they didn't call him Thugg for nothing. At the moment, he was sitting inside of the stolen dark blue Caprice, which he'd parked three blocks further up the street. Since he was turned off onto another street, and pulled close to the curb, he had a direct view of the trap, while the people out selling their drugs couldn't see him.

The thing was, while Thugg wouldn't stand out on the corner and sell dope, he had no problems relieving those who did of some of their extra weight. That's what he liked to call it when their pockets were too fat, and they leaned sideways when they walked. That was the beauty of Atlanta, Ga. These niggaz were super sweet on the jack boy tip because it seemed like their whole life consisted of *flexin*. These niggas loved to be seen. They advertised their earnings like it was already published in Forbes Magazine or something.

"And who am I to disappoint them?" he asked himself. Then he thought about that song by Lyfe Jennings, the one where he sings, "And they be teasing me with these twenty-threes and DVDs in they rides. I be robbin' these niggaz. And if you doing too much, I'm coming to get it."

At that moment, that's how he felt. Thugg reached over to the passenger seat and lifted the black FN Five Seven, a heavy gun that was extremely useful for armed robberies.

***

Monte' looked at the time on his diamond encrusted Jacobs fashion Cartier. He could see that it was later than usual, and he knew that his girl was going to be trippin'. He'd told her that he wouldn't be out too late tonight. The fact that this nigga Juge had gotten a good package was a different story altogether.

They'd learned a long time ago how to pool their resources. Now there were three of them, him, Juge and this other nigga Casper. By themselves, they weren't making any real money. But together, they pooled all of their money and put it into one plate. Then Juge took it to the weight man, and got them their first real drop. That was all just over a year ago. Now they were moving every bit of two and a half bricks. On the next re-up, they should be three or four bricks strong.

So yeah, Monte' wasn't worried about his baby's mama poppin' off at the mouth because he had to put in his own work in order to save his money. *Shit, how she think a nigga can afford all of that fly shit she been rockin'?* Monte' thought as he glanced around.

They were trapping off Line Street, and the business was good. They could have paid workers, but they were all trying to get their weight up before spending money like that, so they were moving their own package. He didn't see Casper anywhere, but that wasn't too unusual. After all, they called him Casper because he moved like a ghost. Casper was from New York, and all of the girls were throwing themselves at him. Country bitches loved them for real city niggaz, especially the way they talked.

Monte' didn't trip on it. Casper was really Juge's partner. Juge was his cousin. Monte' just felt like the nigga could have been out there with them, even if he had gotten off all of his work. But then, too, Monte' was in his feelings. This nigga Casper had fucked some of the same bitches he wished he could fuck.

"Shit." He rubbed both of his hands together, and then brought them up to his mouth and blew warm breath into them.

Juge was standing over by the side of the house, huddled deep into his Starter jacket. He was wearing the Atlanta Falcons red, black, and white one. Monte' was just thinking that he needed to get himself one of those when he looked up and saw the tall nigga walking up the street towards them, swerving, walking like he was drunk or something.

Monte' watched as he stumbled and tripped. He almost went down in the middle of the sidewalk, but somehow caught himself. Then he looked up, directly to where Monte' stood.

"Keep it moving, nigga. This ain't the Salvation Army," Monte' said, as he tried to shoo the nigga.

The nigga made like he was moving.

Juge came out from the side of the house with his 9mm in hand. "What's up, Shawty?" Juge asked. He was looking from

Monte' to where the drunk nigga was almost past them, but Juge's look was like he expected some beef.

"Nah, it ain't nothing, Shawty. Just," he didn't get to finish what he'd been saying.

The drunk suddenly turned towards them, aiming what looked like a hand gun with an extended clip coming out the butt and a laser beam on the bottom of the barrel.

"Nigga," Thugg straightened up and gave both of these niggas the evil eye. "Act like it's Sunday, and praise the Lord," he stated.

"Aww damn, Shawty," Monte' whined like a bitch as he raised his hands to the sky.

But it was Juge that Thugg kept his eye on. The fact that he was wearing one of those clear face masks that distorted the actual facial features, didn't go unnoticed. Juge thought about bringing his gun up.

"Yeah, nigga, drop the heat, too. Jesus don't want no guns up in his church," Thugg told him with a straight face. "And be grateful I don't make you niggaz get naked. It's cold out this bitch."

And again, Juge thought about making a play to bring his 9mm up, but as his hand released the gun, he thought, *it isn't worth it. This nigga looks too serious, and he's wearing a mask. He's not intending to kill anybody.*

As the gun dropped, Thugg saw their submission and smiled. It was always better when he didn't have to body a muthafucka.

***

Later…Thugg was sitting in his charger, which also had nice rims on it. At the moment, he was counting the money he had received from the robbery. He looked up into the rearview as he saw the headlights of the car that pulled up behind him.

Not a minute later, his passenger door opened and he watched as the dark skin, clean cut nigga hopped in.

"Ayo. Peace God," Casper said as he reached across and gave Thugg a pound.

Thugg smiled, dapping the other man up. He'd met Casper about two years ago when he was down in Augusta politicking with some of the Gods.

"Peace, Allah. How you be?" Thugg asked.

"True and living, sun, true and living. But yo, I know you didn't go out bad and miss the stash spot," Casper said, as he saw the money.

He'd told Thugg that these two niggaz had a stash spot under the porch, where they put their money when they got too much. He also made it a point to show off the Cartier watch that graced his arm, not that he didn't have nice watches at home. Thugg just wanted to make sure Casper saw this one.

"Come on, Sun. I'm a thoroughbred, for real," Thugg nodded to the back seat.

When Casper looked, he saw the rolls of money that were wrapped with rubber bands. From what he could see, it had to be about thirty thousand.

"Yo, what I owe you?" Thugg asked, because it was Casper who gave him the easy lick in the first place. Usually, he would have set out and scouted for a nice lick. And truth being told, this was by far the smallest lick that he'd ever hit. On an average day, Thugg was used to getting something like a hundred thousand a lick. Anything less, he didn't think to pull his guns out. He wasn't really into the small time local hustlers. He usually went after big money. When he put his hammer down, it was a hundred stacks or better. But thirty thousand was good. Shit, he didn't have to body anyone.

"Shit, what you feel like? I've still got my loot from my end of the package, so I'm really all good," Casper told him.

Thugg nodded his head. Then he turned and reached into the back seat. He grasped two rolls of money and handed them to Casper.

"No doubt. That's what's up," Casper said.

To Thugg, the money really wasn't an issue because he had money. He had *a lot* of money. So for him, it was really the head rush he got from taking niggaz heart, pride and dignity. Shit, that's how the streets of Augusta bred the best of them. Most niggas screamed *Thug Life* because Tupac made it famous. They tried to live up to a reputation they hadn't really earned. Even some of the niggaz in Augusta, not all of them, were thugs for real. There actually were a few busters in Augusta. But the average nigga couldn't make that statement around him without having to stand on it.

Nah, to him, *Thug Life* was real, and he lived by that code. So he wasn't about to watch it be disrespected by anyone.

Trai'Quan

Chapter Four

Magic City was jumping. The sounds of Kevin Gates could be heard, even out in the parking lot. But when Diane, Juanita, and Alicia stepped inside, it was like they drew all of the attention towards them. All three of them were dressed to impress. Both Juanita and Alicia followed behind Diane as she moved through the crowd. They eventually arrived at the VIP booth, which had already been reserved. Once inside, they were seated. Not long after, there was a knock on the door. One of the bartenders brought in a bucket with three bottles of D'Ambonnay.

"So ow yu two meet?" Alicia asked.

She popped her bottle and pulled out a nice blunt. It wasn't until after she lit it and inhaled that she looked over to Diane.

"I met Juanita after she rocked a cradle," she said.

"Fuck you, bitch. I made a move." Juanita rolled her neck as she looked over at Alicia. "I met a young nigga that was about to become something. One thing led to another, and we hooked up. As fate would have it, Diane ended up becoming his plug."

Alicia hit the blunt then passed it. She held the smoke in her lungs a moment, then exhaled. "And ow yu meet mi uncle?" she asked.

Diane accepted the blunt and hit it deeply. She seem to be thinking about the question carefully before she decided to answer it.

"Big Dredd met my mother when she moved to Georgia. At that point, it was sort of business. I was young then, but he treated me and my sisters like he was our uncle," she replied. She left out the part about how Big Dredd found out that T.J. was stealing from him. And when her mother killed him and the Island boys came, it was Big Dredd who stopped more of them from coming.

Diane turned her bottle up and took a swig. And just as she brought it down, her phone vibrated.

"Yeah," she answered, without checking the number,

"Yo. Where you at. I thought you was in the club," Maine's voice answered.

"I am in the club, nigga. Where you at?" she asked.

"We at the bar," he responded.

She stood up and looked out of the VIP window. "Look up, nigga. VIP box #2," she said, and watched as Maine turned and looked up at her.

"Grab a bottle and y'all come on up," she stated. Then she ended the call.

"Yo oo dat?" Alicia asked.

"Just some of my niggaz. They gon' chill wit us," she explained.

It didn't take long for them to be knocking on the door. Diane stood up to let them in. She hugged Maine, and then his partner, Thugg, as they stepped inside.

***

"This bitch think she's Frank Lucas or Nick Bonds or some shit." Jersey's words were slurred as he spoke, mostly because they'd been drinking and smoking since before they'd hit the club. On top of all the bullshit, they got to the club and found out they couldn't get into VIP. Mutherfuckaz were saying all of the booths were taken.

"Dog, don't let that bitch get under your skin and shit," Burner stated. Since they couldn't get a VIP booth, they'd ended up getting a table in a corner spot.

"Word, word, I smell you, Sun," Jersey said.

But even as he said it, Burner noticed that he kept glancing upwards. It got worse when he pulled out his cocaine pouch and used the little spoon to sniff twice. He knew then that shit could get crazy.

"So, what the homie waiting on? Why we ain't make this move yet?" Jersey asked.

"Dog, sun trying to figure out how much trouble the shit gone be. We murk this bitch, how many mutherfuckaz gone be mad about it?" Burner explained.

"Man, fuck them niggaz. We can worry about that shit later," Jersey exclaimed.

Burner didn't respond. He knew that Jersey was really in his feelings at the moment. He also knew that moving on emotions was stupid, so he didn't say anything. Instead, he pulled out a blunt and lit it.

***

"Yo, Sun, tell me why these niggaz look like they sweating wifey and shit?" Damian asked.

Both he and Justice were seated at another table on the other side of the room. They'd been in the club a good hour before D-Block showed up. But Damian already knew about these niggaz Jersey and Burner. At the moment, he and Justice were too high, having smoked two blunts before they got to the club. Then they'd smoked three more since they'd been there.

Justice looked over at Damian. Then he leaned to the side and looked across the club to where Damian was looking. Since they were both slouched down in their seats, it was hard to actually see them.

"Ayo," Justice began as he reached out to grasp his drink. "I *know* we ain't up in this bitch on some ole stalker shit. Yo. Let a nigga find out."

But Damian wasn't paying him any attention. His eyes were locked in on both Jersey and Burner.

"Nah, I never liked these niggaz, Sun," Damian said. He was quiet for a minute, almost as if he was thinking about something. "I think I'm gon' dead these niggaz," he said.

"Yo. Let a nigga find out you on some old over-protective ass type shit," Justice said. He turned his drink up and hit it strong. Then he reached for the Newport he'd placed in the ashtray. "Yo. So when we gon' do it? Tonight?" Justice asked.

"Nah, nah, sun, wifey ain't give the word yet. But I know the shit coming, though," Damian said.

Justice hit the cigarette.

"Yeah? Let a nigga find out wifey wear the pants and shit. Let a nigga find out," Justice stressed.

***

Thugg was so high that he didn't even realize that he'd fallen asleep lying on the floor in the VIP lounge. When he woke up, it was because Alicia apparently had gone to the ladies room and was coming back. She claimed he was in the way, so she nudged him with her foot and said, "Move," like she was Ludacris or some shit.

He'd been lying on his back with his arm across his eyes, at the time. He removed his arm and blinked. "Huh?" Thugg gave his eyes a second to adjust. Then he looked up at the dreadlocked girl standing over him.

"Yu in de way. Yu need to get up, irie?" Alicia said.

"A'ight. Just chill, love," he mumbled.

Everyone laughed as he got up off the floor and moved to sit beside Diane on the couch.

"Here, nigga. You wanna hit this?" She held out the cherry flavored blunt so that he could grasp it.

Thugg looked at the blunt, then shook his head. "Nah, ma. I need to shake this shit off," he answered.

"That might be a good idea, before my girl get on yo ass up in here," D-Block cracked, and then laughed.

Thugg was still in a daze. He looked across the room at Alicia, who, it seemed, was also looking at him, at the moment. As time went by, he listened to what D-Block and Maine were talking about.

"So these niggaz ain't made a move yet. They ain't said or done nothing crazy either," Maine said.

"Nah, but you know how this shit goes." D-Block paused as she hit the blunt. "Niggaz sit back and talk crazy. Stressing this, I ain't gon' let a bitch punk me, shit. And some kinda way, word gets back to me," she stated.

There was silence for a moment. Thugg's attention was still on Alicia, all five feet eight inches of her, while he balanced out what he thought she weighed. Something like 138 lbs.

"So what about yo goons? You ain't let them loose yet?" Maine asked.

Them niggaz getting on my last nerve," she said referring to Damian and Justice. "I don't know what they got going on with Young Castro, but every time the nigga calls, they disappear for a week or two."

"Knowing them niggaz, they probably doing some body work," Maine suggested.

"Yeah. But this nigga, Young, ain't supposed to be in the game like that. The nigga supposed to be legit," she said.

"Even straight niggaz have issues, ma," Maine said.

***

Alicia wasn't slow. She knew this nigga Thugg was checking her out. And to be truthful about it, she'd been fully aware of his presence since he stepped into the lounge. She just didn't think the nigga was her type. He looked like a rough neck, but he was also a clean cut nigga, rocking his Iceberg jeans, Givenchy shirt, and Ralph Lauren boots. She also noticed the $6,000 Cartier watch on his wrist. Alicia thought, *yeah, he act like a thug, but he dressed like a player.*

She sipped her drink and looked out into the club. She'd just gotten here, and she wasn't about to mess up by getting involved with one of Diane's workers. That's what she assumed these guys were. And what she was looking for was a Boss, not a flunky.

***

"I'm just saying, sun," Justice proclaimed. "If wifey gone let us dead these niggaz, then she needs to come on and let a nigga dead these niggaz."

Damian hit his Black and Mild cigar. His eyes still focused on Jersey and Burner.

"You know what, God?" Damian began. "Shit is like a good song. You can't rush to put that mutherfucka out, because if you do, it won't be a classic. The shit won't be remembered years from now. So the producer has to take their time. Get the shit just right. And when they release that muthafucka." He fell silent, thinking he'd proven his point.

Damian was consciously aware of Justice rolling up another blunt, and licking it so that it would stick. He'd known Justice since they were in the 6th grade, so he knew that his partner was thinking over his every word before he spoke. He knew that Justice thought he was a tender dick for Diane. But he didn't say shit about Justice having a thing for the Mexican bitch, Juanita, knowing that she was with one of Diane's workers, a young nigga named Shine.

"Yo, sun," Justice began. "I fuck wit you. And I fucks wit lil sis. But if a nigga find out that she got you on some ole sensitive, soft nigga shit, I'ma go up side yo melon, sun. Word is bond, I am."

Damian ignored him and kept his focus on these niggaz Jersey and Burner. He still had to get the green light from Diane before he made a move.

***

Burner looked at the message on his phone. It seemed the big homie Swole wanted them to come back home for a meeting. That would put their plans on hold. They were trying to finalize their plans for moving on this bitch D-Block's people. They were really tired of waiting, and then he gets this message. It was almost as if this bitch had an angel sitting on her right shoulder.

"We gotta head up top this week," Burner told Jersey.

"Yeah?" Jersey said. "What's up?" he asked.

"The big homie said he has some info for us. But shiiit, everything should be back on point by next week," Burner explained.

Jersey didn't respond after that. His mind was already made up. He already knew *what* he wanted to do, and *who* he wanted to do it to. Everything else was just them going through the motions.

"A'ight, so when we leaving?" Jersey asked.

"First thing in the morning. That way we can get back before next weekend," Burner explained.

He didn't think they'd need to be up there more than three or four days. Anything longer just didn't make sense. He lifted his drink and took a sip, thinking it really didn't matter. This bitch D-Block was breathing on borrowed time. She just didn't know it yet.

Chapter Five

When Justice rolled over and answered the phone, the last voice he expected to hear wasn't the voice he heard.

"What you doing, papi?" Juanita asked.

"I was asleep, ma. What you got going on?" he asked.

"Not much, just laying across this big ole bed, all lonely and shit. What's up?" she asked seductively.

"I thought you was fuckin' wit' that young kid, Shine. Yo, you know flirting wit' a nigga like me ain't healthy for some niggaz," Justice stated.

"Mmmmhm. Well, me and Shine ain't together no more," she told him. "He got himself a young girl now. We ain't been together like three weeks now."

"Oh yeah?" Justice lifted his Hublot and saw that it was nearly 4:00 am. "What about your kids?" he asked, not that he wasn't gonna pull up. He'd been wanting to tap that ass since he first met her, which was why he was already getting up.

"My son is in college. He's at Morehouse. And my daughter, she really lives with my mother," Juanita told him. "Now what's up, papi? You gon' come through, or what?" she asked.

Justice stood, then walked to his bathroom. The apartment wasn't but a one bedroom spot. He was a street nigga, so he didn't spend too much time there.

"Yo, you out in Woodlake, right?" he asked.

"Mmhm. I'ma text ya the address," she said.

"Ayo," Justice said. "Ya know, it's like early Monday morning and shit."

"Ok. And your point is?" she asked.

"A nigga ain't riding way over there for no quick booty call type shit. Yo, a nigga gone wanna kick back and rest, too. Maybe get some breakfast and shit, ma," he stated. He'd just pulled out his toothbrush and a tube of toothpaste to brush his teeth.

"How you know you gon' be able to eat when I finish wit' you, papi?" she cracked.

"Oh, it's like that, huh?" Justice smiled.

"Yeah. It's just like that. Look, I'm texting my address to you. I'll be expecting you in like fifteen minutes," she said.

"Shiiit. I'll be there in ten," Justice stated.

They ended the call. He'd been having a feeling that they were going to hook up, especially when Diane told him that Juanita had been asking twenty-one questions about him. He just wasn't going to pull up on her while she had something going on with one of Diane's workers. But since that was no longer the issue...

***

In the streets, she was the boss. But in the bedroom, Damian made that ass submit. He lay on his stomach with both of her thighs draped across his shoulders. His head slightly bent to an angle, while his tongue dug deep in her.

"Sss. Oh shit." Diane's breathing was heavy. Her pussy was hot, and extremely wet. He loved her taste because it was exotic, like honey and lemon juice heated to perfect temperature. Damian devoured her and wasn't intending to let up.

Playing with her clit, he knew it was sensitive to the touch, but that didn't stop him from sucking on it and stroking it with his thumb. He was thinking of all the times when she walked around like she was the shit, and had 75% of the city afraid of her, but in this bedroom, she bowed down to his will.

"Ok, baby. Ok. Oooh. Stop, nigga. This shit is *not* funny," she chanted.

But Damian wasn't hearing that shit. And when he was finished putting the tongue down, then he was gon' put the dick down. Righteously. Oh, she was the boss in the streets, but he was the boss in the sheets.

***

Justice bit down on his own teeth as he fed her the dick. He was also enjoying the chase. Juanita seemed to be trying to get away from the dick. But with her thighs spread wide and him planted in the middle of them, there didn't seem to be too many places she could go.

She screamed as he impaled her on his dick repeatedly. It was as if his hips were controlling a jackhammer.

Juanita opened her eyes and looked up into his face as he concentrated on each stroke. His every move inside of her pushed through her tightness and widened her muscles. Her lips parted and her breathing was heavy.

Shine had been a baby. She'd been able to be the one in control, then. But not with Justice. It was as if she'd just broken the law and this nigga was the judge handing out hard time. He was relentless, and not letting up at all. Once again, she screamed. But this time, it was an orgasm.

Justice buried his face into her neck as he felt her walls squeeze him and then release, over and over. Then he pushed all the way inside of her, deep, and unleashed his seed. It was also at that point when he realized he wasn't wearing a condom, either, and didn't know if she was on birth control.

***

Big Steve put the surgical face mask on as he stepped into the lab. He didn't like the smell of crack being cooked. And at the lab, they not only had people cooking crack, they were also making crystal meth and ecstasy pills. The lab was their major spot. It consisted of two apartments in Pinewalk that were side by side. The middle wall was knocked down, making it one large area. All of the doors and windows were reinforced with extra thick steel plating. There were twenty-one women that worked in the lab. All of them handpicked by D-Block.

Big Steve had only been over the lab the past seven months. The way D-Block had it set up, there wasn't any of their product being sold in Pinewalk. In fact, the only hustlers out there only sold weed. D-Block didn't allow for them to sell anything else. Other than weed, you'd find two bootleg houses, and one candy lady. But nobody sold crack cocaine, powder cocaine, meth, or pills out in Pinewalk. And if they did it on the low, they made damn sure D-Block didn't find out.

"What do we have ready to go?" Big Steve asked.

He was speaking to the super thick redbone, who was called Niecey. The bitch was so thick that it was a wonder she wasn't fat. But she was also tall, too.

"We've got Man-Man's order ready to go. By the time you take that out to Butler Manor and come back, both Izzy and Maine's order should be ready," she said.

By doing it this way, D-Block knew there was less of a chance the Feds would get wind of them or where her product was cooked. She didn't even allow any of the known workers to pull up and get their work.

"A'ight. I'ma take that. I'll be back in about an hour. Anybody need me to bring anything back?" he called out.

"Yeah, some food," one of the girls called out.

"Some Michelob Light, and this bitch wants Coronas," another one called out.

44

Big Steve made a mental note of everything they called out, especially the food, because they weren't allowed to leave the lab until their shift was over. D-Block had two 12-hour shifts, with twenty-one women on each.

Big Steve tossed the big Nike nylon bag on the back seat. He treated the black Cadillac like it was his favorite bitch. All of his baby mamas were jealous of the car.

He pulled out of Pinewalk and jumped onto Deans Bridge Rd. As he passed the Regency Mall and went up the hill, he saw that there was a red light up ahead. He slowed down until he came to a stop. He'd just reached into his pocket to pull out his phone when the two big body Chevrolet Suburbans pulled up. One blocked him in from the back, while the other one pulled up beside him, on his driver side.

"What the fuck?" Big Steve didn't know if they were cops or jackboys.

But when the doors opened and four men in ski masks jumped out with their guns aimed at him, he knew.

"Open the door, muthafucka, and come up off that shit." The one with the sawed off pump was at the window talking.

At this time, Big Steve was trying to see if he could get his 9mm from under the seat. Out in the street, cars had started back moving, running the red light when they saw what was going on.

"Open the door, nigga," another gunman said.

"Man, fuck this shit," the one with the shotgun said. *Ka-chink.* He cocked it. *Boom.*

The shot would have taken Big Steve's head off had it not been for the window, but he was definitely dying. His body leaned over into the passenger seat, while one of the gunmen broke the back window with his gun and grabbed the bag.

"Come on, come on. Let's go, let's go."

With a quick glance around to make sure there weren't any cops around, they jumped back into the SUV and both trucks pulled off. Neither one of them even noticed the royal blue Dodge Durango that fell in behind the second Suburban. And that was where their lick went bad. They just didn't know it yet.

Chapter Six
Retribution

There were seven people standing inside of the parking lot of the old jail at 401 Walton Way. It was the most unusual spot to be having the conversation that they were having. These days, the old jail was used to pay tickets and for miscellaneous non-violent charges. All of the felony charges went to the new jail on Phinizy Rd.

When she got the call, Diane was in the building paying a parking ticket she had. Actually, there were 3 of them. But she'd listened while Alicia explained what she saw. Then she told her to meet her at the jail. She'd then called her girl, Charlisa, and had her go check on the lab. Next, she sent out a double 007 to everyone else's phone, and told them where she was. That had been twenty minutes ago.

Juanita pulled up in her SL-class convertible, which was cocaine white. She was the first one there, after Alicia, because she'd already been downtown with her mother. Damian and Justice arrived in his Range Rover, and Main rode with Thugg in his SRT charger. They were the last to pull up.

"Alright. So what happened?" Maine asked.

They all listened as Alicia explained how Diane asked her to follow Big Steve so that she would become familiar with his routes. Diane usually changed that position up about every 9 months. She was about to have Alicia take over the deliveries after Big Steve's time was up, and she wanted her to know how he got to where without attracting the cops.

The only thing was, Alicia didn't tell Big Steve that she was following him. She wanted him to keep acting as natural as he was.

"And you're sure it was Harrisburg that you followed them to?" Diane asked. "They didn't just stop there for a minute, and later went somewhere else?"

"Non, de quashie took de bag in dis ouse. Mi waited, in fact, mi was still der when mi call yu," Alicia explained.

"Who would be beefin' wit' ya from Harrisburg?" Maine was the one to ask the question.

"I don't even know who's up that way these days. Anybody know?" Diane glanced around.

"You know, Jeeta and Young Castro took out the Crips who were up there," Juanita said.

As she spoke, Diane caught the slight glance that passed between Damian and Justice. She suspected they might have had a hand in that, too.

"From what I've heard," Juanita said. "These new muthafuckaz call themselves the Loe Life Mafia. They're the ones who have Harrisburg on lockdown nowadays."

This information caused Diane to look confused. "Hold up. My sister, Brina, has a kid by Trigger. Ain't no way some LOE niggaz violated like that," she stated.

Juanita shook her head at this. "They ain't the same," she said. "From what I've heard in the Hispanic communities on Central Ave, the Loe Life Mafia isn't LOE. There's even some beef between them. This mafia is run by some young guy named Don Angelino. He's originally from Augusta, but spent the past 12 years in the Bronx, N.Y."

Juanita paused long enough to look at Damian and Justice. They were both from New York, too.

"Yo. Brooklyn don't fuck wit' the BX like that," Justice stated in his heavy voice.

"What else do you know about this Don Angelino nigga?" Diane asked. Now she wanted to know everything.

She was in her contemplative state at the moment. Whoever the fuck these niggaz were, they'd just hit her for 1.5 million in work. And that was *not* going unpunished.

"He's like 30 or 31, but supposed to be super smart. Everybody in his crew, who means something, is older than him. He's mixed. His mother is black. His father is Italian. It's his old man who's from the Bronx," Juanita explained.

"Is he affiliated with anything else?" Diane asked. "I know the Bronx has a lot of Bloods and Latin Kings up there."

"Not that I've heard. He hasn't been known to flag no one particular color," Juanita said. "Oh, and he has two main lieutenants, both older than him. One's called Black Money. He's the one in Lake Almstead. And Teflon runs everything else," she said.

"I know this nigga Black Money," Thugg said.

And everybody looked at him.

"Couple of years ago, I was in Phinizy Rd. on a suspected armed robbery charge. This nigga was on the same block with me. I think he had a murder charge, or something," Thug told them. "I didn't talk to the nigga. He's one of those big niggaz, who think they're tough. I thought I was gone bump heads with the nigga, but my moms posted bail before it happen."

Diane thought about everything she'd heard. Then she sighed heavily. "Muthafucka better be glad Young Castro got a bitch on this soft shit," she stressed. Then she looked at Alicia. "Baby girl, you and Thugg go back to Harrisburg and see what you can find out. I want every swinging dick that had something to do with this shit to pay."

She watched as Thugg tossed the keys to his charger to Maine, since they rode together. Then he followed Alicia to her truck.

"Juanita, see what your people on Central Ave know about this Loe Life Mafia. I need everything they can think of." She told the Hispanic woman.

Juanita nodded. But before she left, Juanita pulled Justice over towards her Benz. They had a few words, then he kissed her as she got in the car and left. When Justice walked back over, he saw the way Diane was looking.

"Yo. Don't even ask, sis. Don't ask," he said.

"Mmmhm," Damian smiled. "Let a nigga find out, sun. Let a nigga find out," he laughed, mocking Justice as he did.

"Whatever." Diane shook her head. "You muthafuckaz need to get back on them niggaz Burner and Jersey. I can take care of this shit. But if shit gets hectic, you'll be the first to know."

Maine was the last one standing as they all pulled off. "Okay. So what do you want me to do?" he asked.

"You gon' follow me to the house. Let me park my ride and then we gon' go look into something else."

***

"So, how do you know D-Block?" Thugg asked.

At the moment, they were parked up the street from the house where the niggaz who'd pulled the lick were. The Suburbans were gone. But, from what she said, she recognized three of the ones who did the job.

"Shi know mi uncle. Im in de Federal prison right now," Alicia explained. "Mi was getting in nuff trouble in Florida. So im sent Mi ya to keep outta dem bakra jail."

"Oh yeah?" Thug smiled. "So what were you doing down there, boosting clothes or something? You look too pretty to be doing anything else."

Alicia turned her head and smiled at the compliment, showing off her dimples.

"Don't let di looks fool yu. Everyone knows down der mi guns go boom," she stated.

Thugg took the time to really look at this girl. She had to be just over twenty-five or twenty-six, and like two inches shorter than him. He was 5'10½" that made her around 5'8". But she was definitely thick. It took everything he had to not openly stare at the way her Prada print skirt rode high on her thighs, showing off her mocha brown complexion, as she sat behind the wheel. She wore D&G boots with a two-inch heel. On top of that, she wore a pair of Christian Dior shades with gold frames and blue tint lenses.

"So you want me to believe yo sexy ass is gangsta? Yeah right," he chuckled.

Then watched as she sucked her teeth and smiled. "Nuff respect. Yu ear. Yu ain't seen gangsta yet. Mi ear bout yu. But mi not impressed yet," she stated.

"Oh yeah?" Thug smiled.

"Mi let yu know when yu do something dat impress mi. So don't stress yer self," she told him.

If only you knew, baby, Thugg thought. This was one female he was beginning to like. Most of the time, he wouldn't be into relationships and shit. That was because his taste was different. Thugg was into the type of women like D-Block and her sisters, tough and fine. They knew when to be a lady, and when to back their nigga up. But all of the Blaylock women were taken, so he didn't expect to find too many like them down south.

Truth be told, he thought he'd have to go to Brooklyn or Queens to find the type of woman he wanted to spend his life with. Yet something was telling him that this woman just might surprise him.

Alicia was thinking something similar. She'd had a few flings with a few guys who'd been street niggaz. But even though they had that, which attracted her to them, none of them were consistent, and all of them were hoes. However, she wasn't so sure about this nigga. Diane said he was one of her Street Sweepers. At the club, she didn't see too much in him. But now, something seemed different as he watched the house. Alicia felt a vibe coming off of him, and the only word she could think of to explain it was predatorial.

Chapter Seven

"Nope. See you a stupid nigga," Black Money said as he sat back on the porch, smoking the Cohiba that was packed with weed. This was his specialty.

At the moment, he was talking to Junior and Detroit, who were talking about some bitches they'd met at the Augusta Mall the other day.

"Listen, thug, I'm telling you. The bitch had one of those stupid fat asses. You just had to see the bitch to believe the shit was real," Junior explained.

"Yeah, but the bitch wasn't beautiful, either," Detroit put his two cents in. "You let me tell the story, she might have been one of them fuck niggaz who you see on Ricki Lake and shit," he laughed, thinking he was funny.

Junior twisted his face up. He really didn't like this nigga, Detroit, anyway. He was always trying to act like he was better than everybody else. He was one of those high yellow niggaz, who thought his skin color made him *that* nigga. Junior was thinking, *if it wasn't for the fact that the nigga was Angelino's cousin, I would have been seen about the nigga, murked his ass like yesterday. Fo' sho'.*

"This muthafucka wouldn't know a *bad* bitch if she walked up and told him she was a bad bitch," he laughed. "Nigga, is you a virgin?" Even as he fell over laughing, Junior was aware of the sour look on Detroit's face, but he didn't care.

Behind them, the door opened and Zay stepped out. "Say, Black, Teflon said to tell you to come back there to the kitchen," Zay stated. Then he watched as Black Money lifted his large, 6'6" frame up out of the chair. He was a big nigga all the way around. Not only was he tall, Black Money weighed over 300lbs, but he wasn't obese. At thirty-eight years of age, many wouldn't have known that Black Money had played football at Clemson when he was in college, and that he'd been asked to attend training camp with the Chicago Bears right before he blew his left knee. But that was in his past. Now he was one of the most feared niggaz in the streets, and he loved to fight.

He stepped around them and made his way into the house. It didn't take long for him to reach the kitchen. Once there, he saw Angelino sitting at the table on his phone, while Teflon sat across from him, smoking a cigarette. On the table lay all of the crack, meth, and pills they'd just hit for.

Teflon looked up as he entered. "Big bruh," he smiled.

It was a good thing they'd had Black Money driving the stolen Suburban, instead of getting out, because surely somebody would have remembered him.

"What it look like, thug?" Black Money asked.

"Something like a little over a mill," Teflon said, and then hit the cigarette. "Nephew said we gon' split it two ways, me and you. Let both our teams do what they do," he explained.

Black Money saw that it was divided, too.

"A'ight, and what about retaliation?" he asked.

Angelino held his phone away from his face and said, "If y'all did the shit the way I laid it out for you, shouldn't nobody know shit. It wasn't too many people that knew about that spot. The cops don't even know about it," he said.

They still didn't know how *he* found out about it. Angelino never revealed too much about his moves.

***

When she told him to pull up at the car lot, Maine thought that she was thinking about buying one of the expensive ass cars that were on display. But he followed her as she walked inside, ignored the sales people, and continued to the back. When they reached the door that said *Manager*, Maine expected her to stop and knock. But she didn't. Instead, she opened the door and stepped in. He followed close behind.

Inside, Maine saw the young nigga sitting behind the desk smoking a Torano cigar. There was another nigga sitting on a leather couch, texting on his phone. He only slightly looked up. But the one behind the desk smiled.

"Muthafuckin' D-Block. What's up, baby?" Young Castro asked.

Diane stepped further into the office and looked around. "Is this all you niggaz do all day? While I'm out here doing all the work, you muthafuckaz be sitting up here in the muthafuckin' AC and shit," she ranted.

The whole time Young Castro was bobbing his head. "It's good to see you, too, baby. I take it the young gunner been keeping you happy at home. Loho's your bodyguard?" he asked.

"Maine, this is Young Castro, Castro-Maine," she said.

Maine watched as Young Castro's eyes took him in. "Oh. You the young animal outta Apple Valley. Yo, peace, pah. Welcome to the family," he said. Then he turned his attention back to D-Block. Only this time he was all business. "Okay. So there must be a problem for you to be down here, standing in my office, because I *know* you've been doing good all year. So talk to me," he said.

Young Castro listened as Diane gave him the rundown of the hit on Big Steve, and then everything she'd heard about Burner and Jersey, as well as the fact that she had Damian and Justice keeping an eye on those two.

"And you don't think them niggaz got anything to do wit' the Loe Life Mafia?" he asked, causing her to look at him sideways.

"I never mentioned who these niggaz were. How you know they Loe Life Mafia?" she asked.

"Well, after I had Damian and Justice get rid of the Crips who were running Harrisburg, we thought about setting up something up there," he smiled. "That was before we got too hot and the Feds started investigating us. Long story made short, we gave you the job, went legit, and been clean ever since." He paused. "However, we have been keeping tabs on the streets. When you said some Harrisburg niggaz pulled the lick, that could only be Angelino. But this kid ain't stupid." He said.

"He's far from stupid," Jeeta added.

Diane looked at both of them closely. She thought she might have to be careful with these Loe Life Mafia niggaz.

Chapter Eight

D-Block had to move the lab. The truth was the location had been compromised. Somebody knew that the Pinewalk apartment was the lab. When she'd gone over the details with Alicia, one of the Suburbans had been inside of the parking lot, and had gotten behind Big Steve when he left. She hadn't thought anything strange then, but the truth was, somebody knew what the apartment was. So Diane had it cleared out in three days.

The entire lab was moved to a three bedroom house in Woodlake-2. All of the walls were knocked down, except for the bathroom, and the doors and windows re-enforced. She realized, one of the reasons they hit Big Steve was because it would take an army to hit the lab itself.

***

Two weeks later…

"So what do we know?" Diane asked the question as she looked around the hotel room.

She'd picked this location for the meeting because she wasn't sure who was keeping tabs on her organization.

"I've been watching these niggaz in Harrisburg," Thugg said. "I've just about gotten it down to all of the players, who does what, and where they do it at. A couple of times I could have touched one or two, but you said not to make a move yet."

Diane nodded. After getting the rundown from Young and Jeeta on everything they knew about this Loe Life Mafia and this Don Angelino, she'd come to realize that this nigga might not know who he robbed. Or, someone else had given him a job without the details. Young seemed to think that the nigga wouldn't violate any one associated with him without permission.

"Have you seen any of them with anybody we don't like?" she asked.

"Not really," Thugg said.

"Waat bout dem twins?" Alicia asked.

And from where she sat sideways on the bed, Diane arched an eyebrow and looked at Thugg again. "What twins?" she asked.

Juanita also sat on the bed, and was paying attention to the conversation, while both Damian and Justice were on the far side of the room, not paying attention to the conversation. They seemed to be rolling a blunt and disagreeing about something. Maine sat with one hip on the dresser, listening.

"These two niggaz from Atlanta," Thugg began. "It seems they got shit locked up on Sandhill. But they've met with this nigga Angelino at several restaurants over the past two weeks, and it appeared sort of secret. He didn't take anyone with him. And one time I think he gave them some money. I'm not exactly sure about that."

Diane digested what she'd heard. But, she didn't see the point until Alicia added.

"Mi saw one of these niggaz ride in Pinewalk once," she said. "Not that day, mi think it was on the day when Big Steve was picking up Maine's work."

Now they had her attention.

"Do you know what this niggaz ride was doing there?" she asked

"No. But mi know which apartment dem was parked in front of," Alicia said.

As she called out what apartment, Diane couldn't say she knew who lived there. She looked back at Thugg. "Both of you, see what you can find out about these twins. And find out who they were seeing in Pinewalk. If these niggaz had something to do with this shit, then they gone get the business, too."

After she said that, her attention shifted. They all watched as it seemed like she was about to say something to Damian and Justice, but they were having some type of hushed conversation as they shared their blunt. She just shook her head and turned to Juanita.

"What you got, mami?" she asked. Then she listened as Juanita repeated what both Young and Jeeta had told her, only she had more details and knew a few more things they hadn't said about Don Angelino. It was when she finished that Damian spoke.

"Is it our turn to share?" he asked.

Diane looked surprised that it seemed they hadn't been paying attention this whole time, so she nodded.

"A'ight. The Bloods up top must have gotten a call from somebody, because they told these niggaz, Burner and Jersey, to fall back," Damian said.

"Yeah, but we think they still gon' be a problem," Justice added.

"How y'all know they got a call?" she asked, and watched as Damian looked at Justice, as if they both had a secret.

"Because *we* got a call," Damian said.

"Wait a minute," Maine said. "I thought you niggaz weren't affiliated. I thought y'all were God Body."

"Yeah, sun. Loe are," Justice confirmed. "But up top, some of the Gods got ties wit' the gangs. And somebody heard our names being mentioned in a conversation about a boss female in Georgia."

Justice stopped talking, apparently having said all that he was allowed to say. But he did look to Damian, who sighed before he explained the rest.

"Yeah, ma. One of the Gods realized these niggaz were talking about my Earth, so they put word in this big homie nigga Swole ear." He hunched his shoulders like that alone should explain it. "One thing led to another. The nigga Swole told them not to make a move on you unless it was absolutely necessary. Then the God called me."

After he said that, there was silence in the hotel room for about two minutes.

"Wait a minute." Maine couldn't help but ask, "Who the fuck are you niggaz that you got head gang bangers backing down and shit?" he asked.

Damian relit the blunt and they went back to smoking, as if nothing had happened. Then Justice said, "Yo, we still gone touch these niggaz, though, when the time is right." He let that stand.

Diane shook her head. She already knew that they were going to do whatever they were going to do anyway. If they decided that these niggaz, Burner and Jersey, needed to be touched. Then they would be.

***

Young Castro had explained to her that he didn't want her name being screamed in the streets *too* loud. She was instructed to slow down on her movements and run the business. He let her control all of the drug business he'd established in Augusta. When the boat came into the docks in South Carolina, Young would call her, and the two of them would drive to Hilton Head, S.C. They would check out the product, and she'd have it loaded in her ride. That was part of the deal. The fewer people who knew *how* shit went down, the less people in her business. So technically, nobody knew exactly how much product Diane really had, not even her sisters.

Her baby daddy knew, but Damian didn't get into her business. Since he was the one who dug the hole where she buried her dope, only the two of them knew the location.

Diane was thinking about how much she trusted Damien. After the meeting, he'd given her the details that he hadn't mentioned then, and she suspected that Justice knew he would. It was never spoken out loud that he knew, so she knew that the phone call he received came from his step brother, who'd been God at one point, but became Blood. His brother had been in the meeting with Swole when he spoke to Burner about Diane. He'd later pulled Swole's coat as to *who* they were talking about trying. Swole, having some knowledge of Damian and Justice, called and had Burner and Jersey come to Queens. They were told to stand down.

***

"Where you headed to, Shawty?" T-Ray asked.

They'd been sitting up in the apartment that his girl lived in, playing games on the PlayStation, until Leroy got a text on his phone. Now he was preparing to leave.

"Nah, Shawty. This lil bitch Shawnita want a nigga to come spend some time wit' her," Leroy explained.

"That's what's up, Shawty. Make sure you let Shawty know we appreciate that information, too, Shawty."

As he walked out of the apartment, Leroy was thinking there was no way he was about to do that. Shawnita was really a green bitch. While she was fine, and thought she had all the sense because she had all of the dope boys after her, she didn't understand the dynamics of a city nigga's game.

Outside, he used his key chain to disarm the alarm on his FX35 Infiniti, which was silver with a nice set of rims on it. Leroy hopped inside and started the SUV.

He'd just happened to be over to Shawnita's apartment one day when he saw D-Block coming out of one of the apartments. At first, he didn't think nothing of it. But when he mentioned it to Shawnita, she said there were a bunch of bitches over there who worked for the bitch pushing the Denali. So he'd started paying attention to the apartment, without Shawnita catching on to what he was doing. He'd finally put the pieces together as he noticed that the women were inside for twelve hours. Then another set of women came, and the first ones left.

Then there were the pickups. Someone would show up, go inside, stay a few minutes, and then leave with a bag. Leroy knew right then and there what the deal was. But he also suspected the bitches on the inside had a lot of fire power, so running up in there wasn't a real option. He didn't think that he and his twin would be able to pull a lick off. Nine times out of ten, there would be someone following the driver, so he handed the job to Angelino. All they wanted was a three-way split. With what Angelino gave them after the job, they would make every bit of a hundred fifty thousand. To them, that was a good lick, seeing as they hadn't been the one's to put in the work. They were going to let them Loe Life Mafia niggaz deal with this crazy bitch D-Block.

Chapter Nine

Justice rolled over onto his back and watched as Juanita got up and walked to the bathroom naked. The woman was fine, and had one of the nicest asses he'd ever seen. The mutha-fucka looked like two basketballs perfectly cut in half and placed side by side, not a lump, dent, or sag anywhere. Her body was well proportioned for a woman who was 5'7" and weighed just over 140 lbs.

He had to catch himself because he hadn't been in a serious relationship in some time now. And he really didn't know what this was yet. A few minutes later, he watched as she came back.

"See something you like." She smiled.

"Truth be told," he began. "I'm trying to figure out where we're going with this."

She slid onto the bed and got comfortable. Then she looked into his face. "That all depends," she said, causing him to look curiously.

"Depends on what?"

Juanita took a moment to think about her words before she spoke them. "It depends on if you want something serious or not," she stated. "I mean, I'm cool with what we've got going on now. But if you trying to pull out some ownership papers, then we gon' have to talk about that."

"What's to talk about? If you agree to be my Queen, and I agree to be your King, then it's all said and done," he stated.

"Not really, papi." She smiled seductively. "If we gon' be together like that, then I'm not gon' go for the 'I'll pull up for a booty call' nights. Nah, nigga, that ain't gone be good enough."

"Oh yeah? So what you saying then?" He asked.

"Either we gon' share the same roof, or you gon' have enough clothes over here to stay a week at a time. Ain't no telling when I might wanna hold yo ass hostage," she explained.

He'd already told her that he kept a small apartment, and that he didn't have much in it, except clothes. So him bringing them to her house wouldn't be all that hard, nor would it be complicated.

"A'ight. We can do that," he stated.

"We can do what, nigga?" she asked, trying to be clear.

"If you want, I can bring my things over this weekend, and we'll see how it goes. But yo," Justice paused to look into her eyes. "Me and bruh be on some other shit sometimes. There's gonna be times when we putting in work and I can't get home for two or three days, but that's all business. A nigga don't hoe around. I'm too old for that shit," he explained.

"I already know you and Damian got a lot going on. And if D-Block can be woman enough to accept what he got going on, then so can I," she said. "You just have that ass here every chance you get."

"No doubt, baby. No doubt." He smiled, and was feeling good about the future.

***

"We really don't need to meet like this," Don Angelino said as he approached the other man on the Riverwalk.

Being who he was, and having the image he had, he couldn't help but dress the way that he always did. He was wearing an expensive Louis Vuitton, double breasted, pin striped suit, and Christian Louboutin boots, which was complimented by the Kenneth Cole watch and its many diamonds.

"I was just trying to see how shit turned out, Shawty." Leroy smiled, not dressed half as clean as the mixed black Italian that stood before him.

"Was there any backlash from that hook up, Shawty?" he asked.

Leroy watched as the other man smiled. It looked like one of the evil smiles the joker would give Batman. "What? You mean because you didn't tell me we were robbing Diane Blaylock, AKA D-Block to the streets?" Angelino asked. "Or that she has some close ties to both Young Castro and Jeeta Loc?"

"Uh," Leroy began, with a scared look on his face as he tried to think. "I didn't know about the second part. Shawty, I really didn't know this bitch. Nor do I know who she fucks wit, Shawty."

He managed to get all of that out. Then he waited as Don Angelino gazed out across the waters of the Savannah River. His view overlooked some trees over on the South Carolina side.

"You should really look into who you set out to start beef with in the near future," he said, still looking over the river and the few boats that were on it. Angelino then turned to face the other man. "I'm not really worried about these people. I mean, I've got my own army. But you, on the other hand." He held his hands out, palms up. "Without a good team behind you, going up against this bitch can be hazardous to your health. And I can tell you this," Angelino paused before he finished. "You and your twin won't be enough to stand against what she's going to bring to the table."

Leroy thought over that. He knew T-Roy wasn't going to want to hear something like that. He especially wouldn't like to hear that they should bow down to a bitch.

"I think we'll be alright. But Shawty, since they done moved the cook house, we won't be able to hit them again anyway," Leroy said, almost as if he were disappointed.

He watched as Angelino brushed some lint off his trench coat, and then turned as if to leave.

"You should be happy she moved it. I can guarantee you, had she been hit again, the streets would be running blood red by now." Angelino started to walk off. "And, Leroy, if I were you, I'd find something safe to do. And do me a favor, lose my number." With that said, Don Angelino walked off, leaving Leroy standing there looking stupid. He was trying to figure out how to explain all of this to his twin, because T-Roy wasn't going to like it.

"Bumbo Clat, dem buguy aga muthafuckas," Alicia stated, using more patois in her speech.

She was sitting in the passenger seat of Thugg's charger, while they watched Angelino walk back to his C-Class sedan, which was silver. His driver opened the door for him to get in, and then went back to the driver side and got in. Leroy left a short time later.

Alicia looked over at Thugg, who wasn't starting the car so that they could follow one of them. "A wa da yu?" (What's wrong with you?) she asked.

Thugg realized that the more frustrated she got, the heavier her accent became. At some points, she could actually speak pretty good English.

"Nah, we good," he stated. "There ain't no sense in us constantly following either of them because we know where they're both going. Until D-Block gives us the green light to sweep the streets, we just going through the same old motions," he explained.

"Okay, so wat you and I do now den?" she asked.

Thugg took in the Avirex calf-high body dress that she wore, which was white. He could have sworn that she was wearing a thong, along with the D & G open toe wedges that showed her perfectly painted toenails.

"Naw." He reached forward, started the car, and glanced over at her. "I think I'm going to take you out to eat. Do you have a problem with that?" He didn't think she would, so he smiled as he saw her roll her eyes seductively.

"Yeah. I didn't think so," he stated.

***

"So what yo boy got going on wit' Juanita?" Diane asked.

She'd been sitting back on the couch, relaxed as she watched Damian hunched over the coffee table. He was in the process of packing weed into the apple flavored blunt they were about to smoke. But at hearing the question, Damian hesitated and paused to glance sideways at her first.

"What you mean, ma? You know niggaz don't get off into other niggaz business and shit," he stated the facts.

"Uh huh. So you know they got something going on then," she claimed.

Damian rolled the blunt up, and then licked the paper. He stuck it together, then picked up the lighter off the coffee table, but paused a second as he looked at her.

"I thought they was just fuckin'. But yo, Sun done moved his shit into her lab, so I guess shit serious. Why? You got a problem wit' it?" he asked as he lit the blunt and inhaled deeply. The smoke itself was thick.

Diane thought about that while she watched him hit the blunt a few times. Then he passed it to her.

"Nah. They both grown," she said.

As she inhaled the smoke, and it filled her lungs, Diane thought about what she knew about Juanita. She actually knew more than anyone else knew because Juanita had come clean about her going after Shine so that she could get into Young Castro's loop. She'd seen her brother about to self-destruct and wanted to solidify her own business, so she went after a nigga who was young and she could control.

That got her into the loop. But then, Young Castro took a step back and put Diane in charge. So Juanita figured if she stepped to D-Block woman to woman, then she could get on some real shit with her.

"Ain't no need to worry, ma." Damian accepted the blunt back. "Them two actually make a good couple."

"I'm not worried," she stated.

And she wasn't, just as long as Juanita kept it 100 with Justice. She was really feeling her whole swag. She would hate to have to murk her ass because she wasn't acting right.

"Fuck that shit, nigga. You gon' give a bitch some dick, or what?" she asked, accepting the blunt back, as he blew smoke up into the air above their heads.

"Maybe," he stated. "Ya know a nigga got to get his rest and shit. And that thang don't cool off."

"Whatever, nigga." She stood up, still puffing on the blunt.

Diane was wearing a sheer Donna Karan teddy with matching bra and thongs, all of which were hot red.

"Have that ass in the room in five minutes. And Damian," she said, looking back across her shoulder.

"Yeah, what up, ma?" He looked up, his eyes getting sleepy.

"Don't make a bitch wait. This pussy *is* hot. Fuck around and I'll start wit'out you," she said.

Damian looked up and watched her ass sway as she walked away, hypnotized by the motion.

"Nah, fuck that." He pushed up from the couch to follow.

Trai'Quan

Chapter Ten

"So wait a minute, let me see if I got this right, Shawty?" T-Roy said, speaking to his twin.

They were both sitting inside of a sports bar on Gordon Hwy. While there was a game on the large screens, neither one was paying attention. At the moment, Leroy had finished explaining how things went with Don Angelino.

"These muthafuckas is saying we need to be scared of this bitch, Shawty? Is that what you're telling me, Shawty?" T-Roy asked.

He watched as his brother nodded. But inside, he just wasn't feeling the words coming out of his twin's mouth at that moment.

"That ain't gone work, Shawty," T-Roy stressed.

And then Leroy sighed heavily.

"Shawty, look," he began. "We ain't got to be bumping heads wit' this bitch at all, Shawty. We already getting money up on the hill, Shawty. The bitch ain't in our way. She ain't got no people up there at all, Shawty. So why we gotta worry about conflict with this hoe?" Leroy asked.

He waited while his brother sipped his beer. Leroy could tell that there were a whole lot of thoughts going through his twin's head. The hardest one to deal with, he knew, was that he didn't want it to seem like he was scared of a bitch.

"Let me tell you something, Shawty," T-Roy said, holding his brother's undivided attention.

"It really ain't about the bitch, Shawty," T-Roy stated.

Leroy wasn't buying it. He thought back to when they'd first come to Augusta. They happened to be in the Augusta Mall when the bitch D-Block and a Mexican bitch were in the mall shopping. T-Roy had found an opportunity to push up on her, but they hadn't known who she was at the time, which didn't really matter. She'd brushed T-Roy off as if he were a fly, or a speck of dust, or something. They found out later that the bitch was a *boss bitch*.

"Nah, Shawty," T-Roy continued. "It ain't about all of that, Shawty. You see, Shawty, it's really about business. Look at it like this, Shawty. A bitch like that, hell it could be a nigga, sooner or later, muthafuckaz gone be on some spread out shit, looking for more space to push their shit. And Shawty, once they got control of all the major traps, the muthafuckaz gone come our way, too," T-Roy explained his logic.

But Leroy just didn't see it. From what he knew about the situation, D-Block could have moved to the Hill years ago, especially when the last of the McCoy and Palmer boys were arrested or killed. Tim McCoy's family had held the Hill for years, alongside Shorty Palmer and his family. But the Palmers were in several other locations. Either way, when Tim's family held the Hill, nobody was trying them on some take over shit.

Leroy knew that these Blaylock women had been around longer than them. They could have been set up shop on the Hill.

"I'm just saying, Shawty," T-Roy said. "We'll eventually have problems with this bitch. So ain't no sense in trying to avoid her."

Leroy held his tongue. There was no reason to say anything because he could tell that his brother wasn't in his right frame of mind. What he had to do was figure out where he stood.

***

When Burner stepped inside of Applebee's, he paused a minute to take a quick glance around. Then he spotted the person he was there to meet. So he turned and made his way to where the person sat.

"How you doing, beautiful?"

Nico looked up and gave him a 100 watt light bulb smile. It had been over a month now since they'd first met. And most of their communication had been over the phone.

"I'm fine. Have a seat."

"I almost thought that I'd find your friend here with you." He was talking about Imani.

"Last time I checked, you two did everything together," he added.

"Not everything," Nico laughed. "She's with her son's father. But we're not here to talk about her. So what's up with you? I thought you were in the process of expanding your business."

That was what he'd told her some time ago. At that point, they were looking to have removed the bitch, D-Block. But things didn't quite go that way.

"We're looking into something else right now. That thing I talked to you about seems to be complicated."

"Really?" Nico sounded disappointed. "I thought we gave you enough information to make it happen," she explained.

Burner smiled. Not only was he trying to fuck the bitch, but he'd found out that both her and Imani hated D-Block.

"You did, love. And your information was greatly appreciated. But there are some other issues."

"What kind of issues?" Nico wanted to know.

Both she and Imani had agreed, when they found out who Burner and Jersey's competition was, that maybe they could help them bring that bitch, D-Block, down. If there was one particular bitch in all of Augusta that they both hated, it was that fake ass bitch they called D-Block.

"Truthfully speaking, it ain't nothing you can help with, sweetheart." Burner smiled. "But don't worry about it. That bitch and her whole team gon' get the business, when the time is right. But fuck that, what's up with you?"

From there, the conversation became personal. All talk about D-Block was put on hold.

***

Black Money sat at the kitchen table inside of his girl's apartment in Lake Almstead. The money Lit Zay had brought over lay in stacks, counted out before him. He still had to get the funds from Junior before he could take it to the big house. But Angelino wouldn't be pressing about it. Black Money just wished Angelino had allowed him to ride with him to this meeting. He knew all about these niggaz Young Castro and Jeeta Loc. Their track records were known throughout the whole of the A.U.G. But it was also well known that they'd taken a step back from the street life.

Then again, Angelino hadn't said why he was going to meet with the young gunners either.

Since they did sell exotic cars, maybe he was in the market to buy something new. The only reason Black Money even had bad vibes about it was because some time ago, he'd thought that he would bump heads with Jeeta Loc, back when he had a few issues with the Crips who used to run Lake Almstead. But that had been a long time ago. Now he had the spot, and they ran all of Harrisburg. And right now, business was good, real good, at the moment.

***

"Uh, Boss. There's a guy out here asking to see you."

Young Castro glanced up from looking at something on his computer. "Yo, Pah, I thought I told y'all not to bother me with small shit," he stated, and watched as the guy looked nervous.

"Uh, I assumed this guy is someone important. That's why I came back here," he stated.

This caught Young Castro's attention. It wasn't too often that real important people pulled up like that. "Yo, he a tall brown skin brother with a bald head and a neat goatee?" he asked. It had been a while since Francis came by. *That* would be unusual for sure.

"No, sir. He looks half white or something. And he's got a body guard with him. Sharp dresser, wearing a Fred Perry suit," the salesman described.

Young Castro looked over to where Jeeta paused in texting on his phone and glanced up at him.

"Well, show the man back, Pah," he said.

The salesman left to do just that, while Young Castro sat in silent thought. Then there was a light knock on the door.

"Yeah, come on," he stated.

The salesman opened the door, and then stepped to the side so that Angelino and his uncle, Teflon, could enter the office.

"Well, if it ain't the young Don himself," Young Castro stood and pushed his hand out to shake. "What can I do for you, Pah?"

Angelino shook the other man's hand. Then he nodded his head to Jeeta out of respect. He looked down at the seat in front of the desk.

"May I?" he asked.

"Of course, please have a seat," Young Castro said. Then he waited while Angelino removed his trench coat and handed it to Teflon. He sat down and looked across the desk.

"I'm quite sure that by now you know that my people made a mistake," Angelino stated.

"You mean by robbing the young street queen. Yeah, Pah, we all know it was yo peeps," Young said.

He paused a moment in thought, then continued. "But what me and my mans can't understand is why you would even think about touching our fam. You've got enough respect and business sense that you could have come to us straight up," Young said.

Angelino nodded. "It wasn't like that, bruh," he began. "And without being a rat, I'll tell you as much as I can."

Angelino proceeded to explain how someone came to his people and outlined an easy lick. They gave them the details but left out the most important fact. Not until after the robbery did Angelino find out *who* they were hitting, which wasn't the whole truth. But it made some kind of sense.

"Okay, Pah," Young Castro sighed. "Everybody in this office know we in the Jungle, and the rules are kind of funny. The only problem right now, Pah, is how you gon' make peace with the queen."

"Yeah," Jeeta spoke up. They all looked back to where he sat. "Because I kinda got the feeling that she felt you didn't respect her. And history has shown that she doesn't respond well to disrespect," he explained.

Angelino appeared to consider the words, then he turned back to Young Castro. "I would like for you to set up a meeting. I want to sit down with her face to face. Try to see if we can avoid a war," Angelino explained.

"Yo, Pah, are you sure that's a good idea? She ain't gon' meet up unarmed. And she's subject to be PMSing at any given moment," Young told him.

Angelino sighed heavily. "From where I'm sitting, it's the only way to handle the situation," Angelino confessed. "If I avoid her for too long, I'm afraid something could jump off. And who knows, we might be hurt by it, or she might get hurt. And if that happens, I imagine I'd be getting a visit from you two.

Young Castro nodded. "Yeah, Pah. That sounds about right. So how you want to do it?" Young asked.

"Tell her we'll meet in the back parking lot of the old mall. She can bring two of her people. And I'll bring two of mine," Angelino stated. "Tell her I just want to talk. I come in peace."

***

Long after Don Angelino left, Young Castro was sitting in deep thought, trying to figure the young Don out.

"You think she gon' agree to it?" Jeeta asked.

"Pah, she'll agree, even if it's just to show the young Don that she's fearless," Young said.

"And the killer?" Jeeta asked.

"Yeah, him and his mans might be a problem, especially if she loses it."

They were both referring to Damian and Justice. Both of them knowing that D-Block alone would be an issue. And to add those two in, that meant anything could happen.

Young Castro sighed before he continued talking. "It doesn't matter either way, Pah. I'm just going to extend the invitation and let D-Block do what she do," Young told Jeeta, who went back to whatever he was doing on his phone.

Jeeta didn't think too much about it. The way he saw it, if young said they were going to kill every member of the Low Life Mafia, then he would dust his guns off. So he really didn't care.

Chapter Eleven

Unlike Burner, Jersey really didn't care what the big homie Swole said. He was going to have this bitch D-Block touched either way. He just had to be smart about it. His overall logic was that the bitch simply had too much power. And what power she didn't have, people in the streets gave her. He just couldn't see them being able to get any real money while she was around.

Jersey pulled into the gas station and up next to one of the gas pumps. He turned his car off, and then jumped out. After pushing the pump into the tank, he turned and started to the store. Jersey gave a head nod to the sexy young girl behind the counter. Then he grabbed a bag of chips as he made his way to the freezers. Once there, he pulled it open, reached inside, and grabbed a case of Coronas. Just as he was about to close the door, someone bumped into him.

"Oh, my bad, bruh," the person said.

Jersey felt a sharp puncture to his side. It was quick, but he felt whatever it was pierce his body and then withdraw.

"What...the," Jersey stuttered.

When he looked, all he saw was the back of a tall baldhead brown skin guy leaving. It didn't hit him that the guy hadn't stopped at the register to pay for anything. Jersey felt the spot on his side, and noticed that it was wet. When he looked at his hand, he saw the blood. As the realization hit him, so did the pain.

"Oh shit." He stumbled backward and fell into a shelf.

"Sir, are you alright?" The girl behind the cash register asked.

"9-1-1," Jersey muttered and continued to stumble. He lost his grip on the beer and it dropped. A few of the bottles shattered.

"Please. Call. Ambulance," he managed to get out.

The girl watched as his body twisted and he fell backwards into the freezer door. It was then that she saw the blood. But even as she reached for the phone, she knew it was too late. The blood seemed to be pouring out of his body rapidly.

"9-1-1 emergency. How may I help you?"

Before the girl could explain, the guy fell to the floor. She watched in shock as his body stopped moving and just lay there.

When the police arrived, the girl didn't know what to tell them. She watched as they took the body out of the store. When they looked at the camera, it was clear that the guy leaving the store, whoever he was, knew exactly at what angle to turn in order to keep his face hidden. As they watched, they realized he hadn't touched anything that would leave a print. The police had said that this was a professional killing, not some low level street murder.

She was in shock because she had never seen any killing, not that close up. But they eventually left her alone after two hours of asking her questions. Nevertheless, she knew that she would never be the same.

**

D-Block agreed to the meeting, but changed the location of it. She said the mall's parking lot was too much of a risk. She said a better place to meet was the old cotton factory at the end of Augusta Ave, across the train tracks. She was half seated on the hood of the silver CTS V Coupe when she saw the headlights of the Mercedes-Benz. To either side of her stood both Damian and Justice. She would have brought Maine, but he wasn't good at taking orders.

The Mercedes stopped with about two cars distance between them. Leaving the lights on, the driver stepped out the same time the passenger did. Both men were big, but the passenger was football player large. They watched as the two men looked around carefully. Then the driver moved to the back of the Benz and opened the door.

They watched as the expensively dressed young man exited the car. He stood up straight, and since it was night and there was a light breeze, he pulled his double breasted trench coat closed. Then he turned and walked towards the front of the car. He had both his men wait at the car.

Diane pushed off the hood and had Damian and Justice hang back as she moved to meet the man face to face.

"Ms. Blaylock." Angelino inclined his head.

"I prefer either Diane or D-Block, whichever makes you comfortable."

Angelino smiled at her humor. "Okay then," he stated. "D-Block. First, allow me to offer my apologies."

"Yeah." She sucked her teeth. "You mean for your disrespect? You had one of my people killed. I don't think apologies gone make that one up," she stated.

"Unfortunately, this is true," Don Angelino began as he looked into her eyes. "However, in my defense," he began. "Information was given to me. And this said information was not complete. Your name, nor your organization, was mentioned."

She considered what she was hearing and thought about what Young Castro had told her about this so-called Young Don.

"You know, in this business, there's very little room for mistakes like that," she explained. Then she looked over his shoulder to his two men. "Even people in our line of work have families. I've gotta take care of that guy's family. Instead of it being him, I'll be the one who puts his little girl through college."

She looked back into Angelino's eyes. "How am I supposed to conciliate this child when she asks one day, why her father isn't there?"

Diane watched as the self-proclaimed Don thought about what she'd just said. And she could see that he was actually giving it some serious thought.

"Listen (sigh). I sympathize with you about your loss. And if I had a chance, I would take it all back." Don Angelino spread his hands out in front of him. "I would offer my life. But that would only make things worse. And I'm afraid the drugs have been distributed already."

Diane watched as he hunched his shoulders. She could actually see that he did feel bad about what happened. "Okay, since I hear your part, Italian. And it's obvious that you strive to live my Mafia codes," she stated. "Instead of this becoming an act of Vendetta, or a feud, how about I give you the chance to make it up to his little girl?"

"And how exactly would I do this?" Angelino asked.

"I'm well aware that you won't give me the name of the person or persons who gave you the information you acted on," Diane stated. Although, she now suspected it had something to do with these twins she kept hearing about. "So I have a solution that I think we can all be happy with," she stated.

Angelino gave her a slight smile.

"Oh? Then do tell," he said.

"It's simple really," Diane said. "Instead of you telling me anything, how about you and your people take care of the problem, seeing as they actually used you in the first place. And," she paused a moment for effect. "Whatever this person or persons has, you bring to the table. It'll be given to Big

Steve's little girl. You do that, and you and I have no problem," she outlined.

Don Angelino thought about it. "And should I not take up this offer?" he asked.

Diane hunched her shoulders. She then turned as if to walk back to her car, but stopped. "One way or another," she looked back. "The individual who gave you the information will be found and be dealt with. If you do it, then my people are good with your people. Hell, everybody makes mistakes. We may even decide to do business in the near future. But," she once more looked to his two men because she knew they could hear every word. "If my people beat you to the punch, they may decide that you're a threat, and not an asset. In that event, what am I to tell them?"

With that said, she proceeded to walk back to the car. The meeting was over.

***

The first five minutes of the drive was in silence. Don Angelino was deep in thought, trying to look at it all from every conceivable angle. "So how are we going to handle this nephew?" Teflon asked as he drove.

Angelino didn't speak right away. He was still going over everything in his mind. It wouldn't really be all that hard to get rid of the brothers, especially with them not suspecting that it was coming. There would probably be some backlash. After all, they were gang bangers, and the Bloods seemed to have large numbers.

Then again, he could let this bitch handle her own business. After all, there wasn't any real guarantee that she'd come out on top anyway. "I'm going to take a few days to think about it. The whole situation is not that pressing," Don Angelino stated.

Hearing this, Black Money gave Teflon a curious glance out of the corner of his eye. But neither one spoke on it.

***

Diane looked at the text she'd just received. Sitting comfortably in the back of the Mercedes while Justice drove and Damian rode over in the passenger seat. The text was surprising. "Ahem," she cleared her throat, while looking forward at both of their heads.

"Either one of you killed anybody today?"

As she asked, Damian glanced over at Justice, who in turn hunched his shoulders.

"What's on your mind, ma?" Damian asked.

"I just got a text. Maine says the word is somebody just killed the nigga Jersey in a gas station," she explained.

The car moved on in silence for a while. "Nah, ma. We been wit' you for what?" Damian asked.

"About three hours, Sun," Justice said.

"Yeah, like three to four hours. So when it happen?" Damian asked.

She typed a message and waited. Maine must have been waiting because he hit right back. "He said it happened two and a half hours ago," she read.

"You see, ma," Damian laughed. "We ain't the only two niggaz in Augusta putting in work. Although, I really was planning on that one."

Diane was confused. If it wasn't these two who killed Jersey, the, who was it? The way Maine's text sounded, it wasn't him or anyone else he knew. Yet, she couldn't say who all might have had beef with Jersey and Burner. Speaking of Burner, she wondered what he thought.

***

"I know this bitch don't think I'm something to play with." Burner was huffing and puffing as he paced in the living room of the apartment. He, too, had just gotten word of Jersey's death.

For some reason, he had it in his mind that it couldn't have been done by anyone other than D-Block, even though it wasn't exactly her M.O. They didn't have any open animosity with anyone else in Augusta, which meant that it had to be her.

And the bitch had to wait until the big homie was gon' have to just deal with it, he told himself.

He just couldn't see his partner's death going unpunished. Somebody was going to pay. Now all he had to do was figure out how he was going to go about it. Without Jersey, he was alone down here. And if he called back home for some extra bodies, Big Swole would know something was going down. He definitely couldn't trust the homies from Augusta like that. This bitch had too much power in Augusta as it was, and too much respect. None of them would stand with him if they knew he was going after Augusta's queen. He had to come up with something else. Either way, this bitch wasn't getting away with her disrespect.

Trai'Quan

Chapter Twelve

"The fuck? Nigga think muthafuckaz gon' be under a bitch?" T-Roy mumbled as he whipped the Ford Escape through traffic.

The Escape was what he drove whenever he left Augusta and drove back to the A, mostly because it was low profile. There was nothing stand-out about it.

He turned off I-285, coming off the Atlanta metro perimeter. Then he made all of the turns that came next. When he pulled into the New Eastwick apartments, he saw a lot of the young niggaz out there hustling. T-Roy parked the truck and jumped out.

"Shawty. What's up, Twin?" one of the young niggaz called out to him.

But at the moment, T-Roy was all about his business. He threw up the deuces as he headed towards the apartment. It wasn't like he had to look for it. He'd spent quite a bit of time here before the cops forced him and his brother to relocate. Once he reached the door, he knocked.

"Shawty. I know that ain't Twin, Shawty."

The door was opened by a tall, slender built, light skin nigga, with wavy hair.

"Caesar, what it is, Shawty?" T-Roy greeted. He could hear other voices inside, so he knew some of the crew was there.

"Nigga, don't just stand there, Shawty. Come on in." Caesar pulled him into the apartment.

Caesar wasn't just anybody. He was Don Caesar, one of the heads that sat at the round table when the rest of the Dons came together for a meeting. The Good Fella's held many different titles and names before they actually became a major force in Atlanta. Most of them, like Don Caesar, had earned their position in prison. So when they came home and began to build their own structure, it was usually predicated by who that person had become.

"What's the business, lil cousin?" Caesar asked.

Don Caesar was T-Roy and Leroy's older cousin by five and a half years.

"Shawty," T-Roy began. He could tell that whoever else was there had to be in one of the back rooms, probably playing the XBox or something. "We've got a problem down where we at, Shawty," he stated.

Caesar looked down into the other man's face. Then he twisted his own up. "Shawty, what kind of problem you got down there with them country niggaz?" He halfway laughed at it.

But T-Roy wasn't seeing the humor in it. "This is serious, Shawty. Shawty, ain't nobody laughing. We've got a situation down there, Shawty. And it's about to turn up," T-Roy explained.

The seriousness in his voice caused Caesar to stop laughing and become serious, too.

"Okay, Shawty. Tell me what the problem is. And we'll see what we can do about it," Caesar said.

He then led T-Roy into the kitchen, where they both sat at the table. Caesar listened while T-Roy outlined the problem, beginning with the deal they made with Don Angelino to hit the cook house. Through the whole explanation, the only thing he left out was *who* and *what* D-Block was. T-Roy didn't even mention her name, for fear that niggaz in Atlanta had heard something about her. He gave his cousin the impression that they were about to bump heads with another big dopeboy.

***

Pendleton King Park was a monument park. It was known for the historic things that had to do with the Army, especially with Ft. Gordon being a big part of Augusta's history.

Leroy met the person where the Army tank sat with the sand pit. When he walked around the tank, he found him with his back leaned on the tank, smoking a cigarette.

"MOB shit," Leroy called out.

"WHOA," Micky answered.

Micky had been in Augusta at least two years before Leroy and Troy came down. He'd been sent to live with his father, who lived there.

His mother said that he'd been getting into too much trouble in the A. Since he'd been in Augusta, Micky found his way into Teflon's crew, seeing as Teflon was with his stepsister, whom his father had with another woman in Augusta. Since Micky didn't talk like the average nigga from Atlanta, nobody questioned him being a part of the Loe Life Mafia.

"Shawty. What that shit look like, Shawty?" Leroy asked.

It had been strange when Micky first reached out to him. They'd both been inside of the mom and pop store on Broad Street, and somehow a conversation started. Micky was how Leroy first became aware of Don Angelino.

"I don't think it's all that good, fam," Micky told him. "From what I've heard, this nigga, Don Angelino, met with that bitch, D-Block." He fell silent with that, maybe even thinking that what he said spoke for itself.

"And?" Leroy asked.

Micky sighed. "Shawty," Micky began, this time letting the A come out. "Shawty, the bitch wants you two niggaz dead. Only she doesn't seem to know it's y'all who gave the Don that info. She just gave the Don the option to handle it first, or she would see about it," Micky explained.

Most of that information was gathered while eavesdropping at different doors, but Micky had been able to put the pieces together.

"A'ight, Shawty," Leroy said. "So with her not knowing who it was, did this nigga, Angelino, rat us out?"

"Are you kidding me?" Micky laughed. "This fuckin' nigga thinks he's the *real* Italian mob down here. That nigga ain't telling shit."

"Shawty, if that's the case, then how this bitch gon' straighten something up?" Leroy asked.

"The way it sounds, Shawty," Micky began to tell him. "She want Angelino to tighten you niggaz up as a sign that he made a mistake and it wasn't a personal move against her. But if Angelino don't do it, then she was gone take it as a show of disrespect. And nobody knows how that will turn out," Micky explained.

There was silence between the two of them. Micky could see the worry on Leroy's face. He finished his cigarette and thumped it.

"Shawty, listen. The bitch just put them against y'all, Shawty," Micky stated.

Then clarity came in volumes. If Don Angelino didn't hit them, then the bitch would hit the Loe Life Mafia.

***

"I've got a few soldiers I could send back with you, cuz," Don Caesar said. "It's like three niggaz," he continued.

"That ain't gone be no problem for you, Shawty?" T-Roy asked.

"Not really, Shawty. These niggaz Juge and Monte' done had some bad luck anyway. They could use the new scene in order to get right. And Lil Marcus is a trigger happy young nigga. He needs to leave the A for a while anyway, before he gets hot," Don Caesar explained, which was something T-Roy did understand.

After all, it was because he had become trigger happy that he and his twin had to leave the A. He was just hoping that this nigga Lil Marcus wasn't one of those uncontrollable types.

***

"Gurl, I am not feeling this shit," Imani said as she hung her phone up.

She'd been trying to reach Maine for an hour now. But all of her calls kept going to voicemail. She knew that it had something to do with this bitch, D-Block.

"Bitch, I been told you that you should have checked his ass." Nico twisted her head upon her shoulders.

"Mmmhm. Don't worry." Imani pushed her phone back into her pocket.

They were both walking through Wal-Mart. Neither came to buy anything particular. Wal-Mart was just the spot to chill these days.

"What's up wit' that nigga Burner? I thought his ass was gone crush this hoe," Imani asked.

"Gurl, I think that nigga done left Georgia," Nico said. "After his partner got killed, I ain't been seeing his ass."

That really didn't sit right with Imani. She really had been looking forward to Burner and Jersey getting rid of D-Block. That would have made her life a whole lot easier.

"Well, if that muthafucka don't do the job, I'ma have to find some other way to get rid of this bitch," Imani said.

She wasn't really expecting Nico to have any feedback. In fact, Imani was thinking about the fine ass bouncer she met at the club just last week. His name was Jackson. He had mentioned that he worked at the club when he was off duty. He said that he was with the Richmond County GBI, and that he was also a part of a drug task force.

Imani smiled to herself as an idea began to form inside of her mind. If she couldn't get Burner to kill D-Block, maybe she could use this cop, Jackson, to do it. It didn't matter to her one way or another, just as long as the bitch was dealt with.

Chapter Thirteen

The fact that he had some mental health issues wasn't that much of a big deal to him, after all, Maine thought as he turned into Cherokee Plaza and glanced around. He didn't see his baby's mother's ride anywhere, and he knew that she was supposed to be here. Not seeing her BMW X5 anywhere, something told him to look for the little Nissan coupe that her friend, Nico, drove. And sure enough, his eyes located the little blue car parked at the far end of the parking lot. But then he did a double take. Nico's car was parked next to the smoke grey Infiniti Qx56. Even before he was close enough to see the New York tag, Maine knew who's ride it was. What he couldn't figure out was why Nico would be parked next to this nigga Burners' ride. The shit couldn't just be coincidental. But just in case, Maine found a spot on the other side of the parking lot. Pulling his Navigator up alongside of a U-Haul truck, he knew that he wouldn't be seen unless someone was looking for him. So he decided to wait, and see what was going on. And he had a bad feeling about it, too. Something wasn't right.

***

Nico was feeling herself. It wasn't every day that she found herself in the presence of a real baller, one that only had his eyes on her. At the moment, she was laughing at something that Burner said. They were sharing a table inside of a restaurant. Having gone over his plans already, Burner had just told her that he'd called in some favors. He had some people that were on their way down to Augusta. But he wouldn't say much more.

"Well, I'll be glad when this shit is all over," Nico exclaimed. "We're so damn sick of this bitch," she stated.

Then she watched as Burner smiled from across the table where he sat. He really didn't understand how this bitch even crossed paths with a bitch like D-Block. From where he stood, they seemed to be in two different circles. Nico was a fancy hoe who needed a nigga to take care of her, while D-Block was a hood bitch that should have been born with a dick, instead of a pussy.

"Don't even worry about it," Burner said. "Everything go right this weekend, that bitch won't be no more than a memory," he laughed.

Burner hadn't called a team from New York, even though he knew Swole would hear about it eventually. He just didn't want anyone telling him what *not* to do. So he'd reached out to some of the Sex Money Murder homies in Philadelphia that he was cool with.

They were sending a crew down, which was scheduled to arrive the next day. Then, he was going to see what this bitch, D-Block, was really built like.

***

Maine watched as the couple stepped out of the restaurant, laughing about something. He subconsciously wondered if they'd seen him when he first drove through the parking lot. But then he brushed that thought aside. Right now, he was trying to hold his temper in check. He just couldn't believe this bitch was sleeping with the enemy. He knew that neither Imani nor Nico held any love for D-Block. There had been a number of times he'd had to prevent something happening between them and her. He just never thought this bitch would be down with the other team.

Then he stopped thinking for a second. Maine watched as the couple stopped, and stood between both their rides, talking.

"Wait a minute. Where's Imani?" he said, even though there wasn't anyone else in the SUV to answer him. The sound of the question being spoken out loud seemed to make so much sense. Imani had left earlier saying she was going to hook up with Nico. They were gonna chill and get their hair and nails done today.

They usually did that in Cherokee Plaza. But he didn't see Imani's ride anywhere. So where was she, while this trifling ass bitch laughed it up with their enemy?

***

Imani was far from Cherokee Plaza. In fact, she didn't want anyone to happen upon her while she did what she was doing. She looked across the table she sat at inside of the waffle house and into the eyes of the man. Seated, he didn't look 6'3. But he was still handsome, with his clean cut hair, and the 360 waves going around. His skin complexion was a mild brown. Since he wasn't dressed like a cop, it would have been hard for the average person to guess that he was one.

"So, let me see if I understand this correctly," Jackson stated as he looked across the table to the younger woman, whom he'd met at the club one night. He was trying to see the logic in what she'd just told him.

"Your baby's father is best friends with one of the biggest drug dealers in Georgia. He doesn't sell drugs himself, and you want to get this D-Block person out of his life?" He asked, and watched as she nodded her head.

"I'm surprised you haven't heard of D-Block yourself," Imani said.

"Well, I've only been on this GBI drug task force now for a month. I'm still kind of new to it. But if this guy, D-Block, is as big as you say, then I'm quite sure I'll be able to find out all I need to know about him," Jackson outlined.

Then he watched as her face looked confused. "I thought that I told you," Imani said. "D-Block isn't a man. D-Block is a woman."

"A woman?" Jackson asked skeptically. "And this *woman* is a big drug supplier here in the city of Augusta, Ga?"

Imani nodded her head vigorously. But at the same time, she could sense that he was finding it hard to believe her story.

"Forgive me if it seems like I don't believe what you're saying," Jackson began. "I mean, I'm not really from Georgia. And where I'm from, up in Memphis, I've never heard of a woman having that kind of action. I've been in Augusta a year, and I haven't heard anything like that," he explained.

"Okay. I tell you what," Imani began. "You go back and ask the people you work for if they have heard of D-Block. And if you decide that you want to hear the rest of what I know, then you call me."

She gathered her purse and stood up. There was no reason to continue the conversation. But she knew he would call her.

***

Burner opened the door and stepped into the house. He stepped over one of the junkies that was lying out on the floor. Another one was stretched out on the couch, nodding from the dope he'd just shot into his arm. In the distance, he heard the toilet flush and turned just as the door opened down the hall. When Helen stepped out of the bathroom, Burner, once again, had to remind himself that she, too, was a junkie. To just look at her, you couldn't tell. Helen showed none of the signs, like the other junkies lying around her house.

"Bout time you showed up." She smiled, and he saw the only tell-tale sign of her being a junkie. Helen's teeth were rotten and held a dark yellowish stain. But if she didn't smile, no one would know. The woman had a body like Cardi-B.

"That money must be building up," he stated.

Helen ran this trap house for him. Not many dope boys would trust a smoker to run their trap house, but when they met Helen, she was already trappin' out of the house. That was how she kept dope to smoke, and paid her bills. He knew as long as he kept her able to smoke, and kept her bills paid, then she wouldn't mess up his money. Plus, he never left her with too much money for too long.

"Yeah. Hold up while I go get it," she said.

When she turned to walk back to her bedroom, Burner walked to the kitchen. Once there, he opened the refrigerator. Inside, it was full of food. It was a wonder she was able to keep junkies from eating it. But then, too, they knew the food was for her three kids. Helen would nut the fuck up if anybody disrespected her kids. Burner reached inside and grabbed a beer.

"Here you go, daddy," she spoke as she, too, stepped into the kitchen. She held a hand full of money, which she handed him.

"Thanks, love. You about ready for a re-up yet?" Burner asked, which was really why he'd come over. He wanted to make all of his runs before the Sex Money Murder niggaz got there because he might not have the time once the shooting started.

***

His name was Jackson Anthony. A funny name to most because one would think that the last name would be the first, and the first would be the last. But that wasn't the case. His father's last name was Anthony. It was his mother who named him after her grandfather, whose name was Jackson. So he grew up with a lot of kids picking on him about his name. He eventually learned to drown it out and ignore the jokes. He made it through school, college, and the Police Academy.

Jackson thought about all of that as he stood, gazing out of his office window. The office wasn't his alone, it was one he shared with the rest of the Special Drug Task Force Unit or SDTFU.

At the moment, he'd just left the lieutenant's office, having asked about this woman, Diane Blaylock, AKA D-Block. He hadn't believed it when the woman, Imani, told him that this D-Block character was as big as she said. But he'd just heard enough from his lieutenant to know it was *real*. From what he was just told, there was someone else behind her, though. A guy named Casey Porter, whom his lieutenant said was known in the streets as Young Castro.

The problem was that there was a "Do Not Approach" stamp on this guy. All he was told was that if they couldn't catch Porter holding a kilo or better in his hands, they were not to arrest him on drug charges. Period. The same was nearly said about this woman, D-Block, except she was also known for allegedly killing a lot of people. But there was never any proof or witnesses to stand up in court, so they'd never been able to touch her either. Speculation was that Young Castro put this woman into power because she knew how to avoid the police.

Jackson was trying to figure out how he was going to bring them down.

Chapter Fourteen

"So what have we got?" D-Block asked as she drove in and out of traffic.

"These niggaz in Harrisburg ain't make a move yet," Maine spoke from where he leaned against the passenger door. "You said they were going to take care of that business. But from what Thugg told me, these niggaz ain't moving like they had a deadline," he explained.

After her meeting with Angelino, she'd pretty much told her people to fall back. In all honesty, and from what Young Castro and Jeeta told her, she wanted to see if this guy was really about business and maintaining good relations.

She sighed. "Just once, I'd like to meet one of these niggaz who really knows how to run an organization," she said, mostly to herself.

Diane continued driving in silence, but her mind was working overtime. She didn't want to call her sisters in to help her on this. Both of them had gotten out of the game and were raising their kids. Besides, she didn't really need them. She still had her *street sweepers*.

"So tell me, what do you think?" she asked.

Out of the corner of her eye, she could see him grit his teeth and grind them. Diane, more than anyone else, knew firsthand about his mental health issues. She had seen it on more than one occasion.

"Truthfully," Maine began. "I don't think that young nigga likes taking orders from a woman. The nigga tells other niggaz what to do. That ain't the type of muthafucka who takes orders."

Diane kept silent a moment. She'd also had the same thought about it. But before she could speak on it, she was pulling into the driveway of the new cook house, which was located in Woodlake 2. It was currently being run by Alicia. Diane had stepped back and allowed her to run it the way she wanted. She almost thought it was a mistake.

She parked behind Alicia's blue Durango, and they both got out. Upon reaching the door and knocking, it was then opened by one of the girls named Tina.

"D-Block, hey, what's up, girl?" Tina smiled.

"Where's my girl?" Diane asked.

"Who, Lady Dredd? That bitch in the bedroom talking on the phone to yo boy," Tina said. The last part was to Maine.

It wasn't a secret that something had developed between Alicia and Thugg.

Diane turned to him and said. "Stay out here. I'll be back." And she left him in the living room.

This cook house was set up different from the last one. There were three bed rooms, two baths, a living room, and a den, along with the kitchen and pantry. It was the kitchen and den that were used to cook. The first bedroom was where everything was prepared and packaged.

Diane found Alicia in the last bedroom. She was laying on her back, smoking a blunt as she talked on her cellphone. Alicia looked up when Diane stepped into the room.

"Ol' up. Let mi get back wit' you later. De boss jus walk in." Alicia ended her call.

Diane glanced around the bedroom. Instead of moving out into an apartment of her own, Alicia had moved into the cook house and taken this bedroom as her own. She'd said that it was better that way, easier for her to watch the house.

"How's everything going?" Diane asked.

"Every ting good. Wat up?" Alicia returned.

"Trying to figure out how I'm gon' deal with these muthafuckaz who hit the last house," Diane said.

"Pissh. Just kill 'im," Alicia said nonchalantly, as if it was common logic. "De all responsible. De ones who do de job and de ones who tell im bout it. I be de one decide, machine gun im all," she explained.

Even if she hadn't said it, Diane was already pretty much feeling like that was the only solution to the situation.

***

Thugg pulled into the gas station across the street from M & M Schott. He pulled up next to the pumps and stepped out of his Charger. He put the nozzle into his tank, and then turned and walked to the store. He was still thinking about some of the crazy shit Alicia had said. He was so caught up in his thoughts that he nearly over looked the nigga standing at the counter. He was in the process of putting his game down on the girl behind the register. But as Thugg walked past him, headed to the freezers to get an Orange juice, he was more than sure that this was one of the niggaz he had robbed. He just couldn't remember when and where right off. That is, until he heard the nigga talking to the girl.

"Shawty, listen, Shawty," he was saying. "I'm just trying to see if I can make yo dreams come true, Shawty." Juge gave the girl a smile.

"Nigga, how many other bitches ya done spit that same game to?" the girl asked.

"Shawty, a real nigga gone always spit real shit to a real bitch, Shawty," Juge stated.

Thugg opened the freezer, and reached inside for one of the drinks. When he turned, his eyes scanned the parking lot through the window. When he'd robbed this nigga up in Atlanta, there had been two of them. He didn't count Casper. Then his eyes spotted the black Navigator that was parked in front of the phone booths. He couldn't see inside from the distance because the windows were tinted.

As he walked up to the counter, Thugg was trying to figure out what this nigga was doing in Augusta? What were the odds of them finding out the nigga who robbed them was from Augusta? At the counter, Playboy stepped to the side and the girl rang the juice up. Thugg didn't speak. He wasn't sure if this nigga would know his voice or not. So he paid and then stepped outside. He paid for the gas with a credit card by sliding it through the slot. Then jumped back into his charger and pulled off.

The only thing was, he needed to see where these niggaz were kicking it. So he drove into M & M Schott across the street and waited. He found a good view of the gas station, one where he wasn't in clear sight. Then he waited, patiently, like he always waited on a mark.

***

"Hey. Mr. Smooth talker," the girl said, pulling Juge out of his thoughts.

He didn't know what it was, but something about the nigga who'd just walked out of the store seemed familiar. He just couldn't put his finger on it. He watched the nigga walk all the way to his car. Even the way he leaned as he walked seemed familiar.

"Huh? Oh, my bad, Shawty." Juge pushed the thoughts away.

This was his first time in Augusta. He knew that he didn't know anyone else there, so he chalked it up as his mind playing tricks on him. He went back into talking to the beautiful woman behind the register. Five minutes later, there was an echo of thought in his mind.

"Nigga, drop the heat, too. Jesus don't want no guns up in his church."

The memory came out of nowhere. For a second, Juge wondered why all of a sudden he was thinking about the robbery.

***

Thugg followed the Navigator all the way up to Lake Almstead. He kept a few cars between them so that they didn't become aware of his ride. Once there, he parked further up the street and watched as the nigga from inside the store got out along with three other niggaz. One of them was the nigga he'd been hustling with up in the A. They all went into one of the apartments. Since he didn't know anybody in Lake Almstead apartments, he couldn't say who lived there. But one thing was for sure, these niggaz damn sure was too up close and personal for his comfort. He needed to find out why these niggaz just happened to be in his city.

Thugg pulled his phone out and dialed a number. "Yooo. Peace to da God," Casper spoke. "Peace, Sun. Ayo, them two niggaz you lined me up with, where they at now?" he asked.

"Shit, God, last time I saw them clowns, they was on some old GF shit. That's some gang shit. I think it comes from prison," Casper said.

Thugg thought about that. He'd been locked up on Wright St. one time. So he knew all about the Good Fellas, or as some called it, the mob.

"A'ight, God. I was just wondering if them ducks had gotten they feet wet again." Thugg laughed to play it off.

"Nah. But I might have something else for you in about a week or two," Casper said.

Not long after that, they ended the call. Thugg was still beating his brain, trying to figure out why these guys were in Augusta. Then the door to the apartment opened and two niggaz stepped out. That's when it all started to make sense.

Thugg found himself looking at one of the twins that were responsible for the hit on the cook house. He was talking to one of the niggaz who'd just been in the Navigator.

"These bitches done went and got some back up. Huh?" He spoke to the air as he watched the two niggas talk.

Seeing as he still had his phone in hand, Thugg went ahead and dialed another number.

"Yeah. What's the news?" Maine asked.

"I'm sitting up here in Lake Olmstead apartments. I'm watching these twins kickin' it with some Atlanta niggaz. Looks like they're building their team up," Thugg reported.

There was silence on the other end of the line for a moment.

"This shit look serious?" Maine asked.

"Maybe." Thugg didn't mention that he already had history with two of them.

"Alright. Let me see how sis wanna handle the situation," Maine stated.

As the call ended, Thugg wondered how that was going to play out. They all knew that D-Block had given these Loe Life Mafia niggaz the choice of straightening their face, or being put on the same plate as these twins. Either way, it didn't matter to him. Whoever got the business end of his .45, just got it. He was really hoping D-Block would be smart enough to take all of these niggaz out, both the Atlanta niggaz and the Loe Life Mafia niggaz. It wouldn't make sense if they killed some and left the others breathing.

Chapter Fifteen

"So how do you want to do this, bro?"

Burner looked across the table to where One Blood sat. It was kind of funny to him. At the moment, they were sitting inside of Sonic's and Burner was trying to figure out how this light skin, pretty boy was the Big Homie over a Sex Money Murder set. Other than him looking like he should be a clothing model, this nigga was too young to be a Big Homie. He couldn't have been twenty-three, if that. But sure enough, One Blood was who his mans sent to help him, along with the other five members of this set, who were left at their motel up on Washington Rd.

"From what you've told me," One Blood continued speaking. "These ain't no free pick street niggaz. And they ain't a gang. But what you haven't told me was how much difficulty to expect."

Burner lifted his cup. He could hear the ice rattling around inside. This meant his soda was about gone. He brought the straw to his lips and sucked on it. He swallowed, then spoke.

"First of all, this bitch got a whole team of killers. Getting to her might not be too hard. She rides around Augusta by herself, like she's the muthafucking Queen of the City," he stressed, his words holding plenty of disdain, contempt, and hatred for D-Block. "But even that don't mean the bitch gon' be easy to take out. This bitch is like some type of G.I. Joe bitch under pressure," he added, which, unbeknownst to him, was closer to the truth than he realized.

"A'ight, homie. Let me do my homework for a couple days. Just tell me everything I need to know about this bitch. When I'm done, I'll let you know how it's going down," One Blood said.

Even though he was so young, and a pretty boy on top of that, Burner was hearing how he spoke. He was thinking maybe there was a reason this nigga held the position that he held in his set.

***

The first thing she did every morning when she woke was go to the gym. Not the public gym, but the one that Damian had built behind the house. It was an extra feature he'd had added on, no larger than another den. Inside was everything needed to keep in shape. Diane made it a point to spend an hour in the gym every morning, which was why she always woke up an hour and a half before everyone else. Training had her used to waking up like that.

She went through one of her regular routines. Today it was lower body and abs. This consisted of squats, lunges, leg lifts, and sit ups. She'd be doing a total of ten sets of each.

It was during her tenth set of sit ups that she had a flash-back of when she'd been a Navy Special Ops Operative.

After her and her sisters helped their mother kill the Island boys who'd come to Augusta, Diane was sure the police would find out, especially since she'd known so many on the school bus that day. So when she turned seventeen, a couple of months later, she'd dropped out of school, took and passed the GED test, and enlisted in the Navy. The whole thing was her attempt to avoid the police for the murders.

She'd never expected to learn that she was so good at it. After her first year of basic training, someone had taken notice of her. The way she put in more energy than the others during physical training exercises, the way she paid attention, and es-pecially how she shot a gun. Diane was then recruited by a

Black Ops Navy Seal Lieutenant. Apparently, they had a mission that wouldn't be successful without the aid of a woman. And they couldn't risk using a civilian.

Diane Blaylock was brought in at the age of eighteen, and they completed the mission, followed by many more after that. Her Black Ops team wasn't famous or known, like Seal Team 6 or any of those, because the missions they went on were the kind that never got spoken of. His team specialized in High Security Clearance Missions, which pretty much meant sanctioned assassinations.

For four years after her first year joining, Diane had performed these actions nearly perfectly. Then she met a US Army Delta Force Officer by the name of Damian Chapman, known to his team as DC, and somehow they'd had chemistry.

Diane finished her workout and looked at the time on her watch. Twelve minutes after 6am. Now she needed to take a shower and feed the kids. After that, she'd be on D-Block time, business as usual.

***

"Bitch, what happened to you?" Nico asked. Holding her phone to her face as she used the other hand to dig around inside her purse. She was at the counter inside of IHOP, about to pay for her food when Imani called.

"I had some shit to do. But I think it's all good now," Imani said, omitting the fact that she'd met with a police officer to try and have D-Block put away. Snitching wasn't something to be discussed openly.

Nico paid the girl behind the register, then took her food, and found a table.

"Well, I talked to you know who and he said it's still going down," Nico stated.

She nodded and smiled at the bald head well-dressed black man who sat in the booth next to hers. If she hadn't been so hungry, she might've flirted with him. Or so she thought, until she got a glance at the wedding ring.

"But how is he going to do that with his partner gone?" Imani asked.

"Oh. Gurl, this nigga is resourceful. He got some Sex Money Murder niggaz from Philly to come down here and help him. Shit. They already making plans on how to get it done," Nico explained.

As she spoke, Nico also began eating her food. She listened as Imani changed subjects and they talked about something else. She'd completely forgot about the older brown skin man seated behind her.

Nico was so caught up in eating and talking that she didn't notice the brown skin, bald head man as he finished his meal. Then he stood up and left. His entire movement was inconspicuously made.

***

Nico was in the process of texting something to Burner as she walked out of IHOP and towards her Chevy Equinox. At the moment, they were making plans on when and where they were going to hook up later on that day. She laughed at something he said as she opened the door and slid into the driver seat.

Nico was just about to say something in response, when she caught a flash of something in her rearview mirror. But before she could turn to look, the garrote cable slipped over her head and settled around her neck. The cable was then pulled tight, preventing her from breathing. She tried to fight, but because of the space being so small, there wasn't much room to move. She could feel the asphyxiation as the person strangled her.

Nico beat her hand against the window, hoping it would break. Then she tried reaching back to scratch the killer's face. But nothing seemed to work. Then she felt the life slip away from her. A few seconds later, she stopped thrashing and moving, her body went still.

Once he was sure she was dead, the killer reached over the seat and grabbed her phone. Then, with a careful look around the parking lot, he exited the SUV and calmly walked away.

As the killer drove away, he went through Nico's phone. He read all of her texts. And added that information with what he'd overheard while inside of IHOP. He realized he'd moved just a little too slow. Burner should have been removed immediately after Jersey. Instead, he'd had the time to bring in some more people, which would only make the job that much harder. Now he not only had to kill Burner as soon as possible, but he had to kill the people he'd brought in.

The killer sighed as he texted a message to Burner's phone from Nico's phone. The best part about killing her in the SUV was that she had real dark tint on the windows. It was possible the SUV could sit there a day or two before someone noticed, which would give him the time he needed to get Burner, and possibly his team, too.

Trai'Quan

Chapter Sixteen

"You're going to have to make a decision sooner or later, nephew," Teflon said, walking into the den, which Angelino had made into a study.

One wall alone held books, everything from Malcolm X, Message to the Blackman, and 48 Laws of Power to the Art of War and the Chinese Analects. When Teflon walked in, he wasn't surprised to see his nephew sitting in his recliner reading Robert Greene's book *Mastery*. He waited, while Angelino read the last of the page he'd been reading, and then watched as the younger man closed the book. He then sat it on the table next to him. Angelino looked towards his uncle, and watched as he moved to take a seat across from him on the comforter.

"And you're referring to the words spoken by the young female. That I do something about the one who gave me the information on her operation," Angelino said. But he didn't follow through immediately. Instead, he appeared to contemplate the whole issue seriously.

Teflon, on the other hand, suspected that Angelino already knew what he was going to do. It was more a matter of execution now.

"The first thing is," Angelino began. "I rarely jump when my mother tells me to do something. What makes ya think I'll jump because this bitch said that I should jump?"

Teflon half hunched his shoulders as he listened to his nephew outline the reality.

"And on top of that," Angelino continued. "I never make a move without carefully considering all of the angles."

To this, Teflon nodded. This part made sense. He knew personally that his nephew wasn't reckless, which was one of the reasons he chose to follow as the young man led.

"But at the end of the day," Don Angelino said with a completely straight face. "What makes you think that I haven't considered falling back, letting this bitch solve her own problem? That would allow us to come in and clean up the mess, which could quite possibly give me the edge over every single organization in Augusta."

This time Teflon looked at him through those types of eyes that asked questions. The question they were asking at that very moment was, is this a good course of action, especially considering *who* this bitch was associated with? And he said that.

"And you've considered the possibilities of the war that could come about because of such an action?" Teflon asked.

He waited, while Angelino tilted his head as if in deep thought.

"I have," he said. "And I've also come to the overall conclusion that without her Street Sweepers, she's not that much of a threat. We remove them from the picture, and she can't hold the streets herself," he said.

"Nephew," Teflon began. "I give you a lot of credit for being one of the smartest young niggaz I know. But right now, it seems like you're seriously underestimating the situation."

"Yeah?" Angelino said. "Then why don't you go ahead and explain it to me, uncle."

Teflon didn't exactly know where to begin. "Nephew, we ain't even gotta go too deep into it. Do you think these niggaz, Young Castro and Jeeta, ain't gone come out of retirement for this bitch? And if they do, there'll be a whole lot of blood spilled," Teflon explained.

"I've been considering that. And," Angelino said. "It's the part I'm trying to figure out now. If I can get a handle on that, then we take control of Augusta."

That is a pretty big if, Teflon thought. They all knew the history of these two, and the rest of Young Castro's crew. Poe and Cream, then there were the sisters, Sabrina and Vanessa Blaylock, all of whom stepped out of the game on good terms. But when they were in it, they were a force to be reckoned with. Making the question now, what was his nephew really up to? Was he putting the good of the family on the back burner, just to prove a point? Or was he thinking that they really had a chance at this?

***

Both Thugg and Maine were trying to figure out what these niggaz from Atlanta had going on. They sat in the dark grey Lincoln MKZ sedan, parked up the street. They were far enough away that they could watch Lake Almstead and not be seen easily. A person would have to literally walk up on the car to see them inside.

"So who ya think these niggaz down here for? Us or these Loe Life Mafia niggaz?" Maine asked.

That had been the thought running through Thugg's head since he first saw the niggaz in Augusta.

"Depends," he stated. "Do ya think them Loe niggaz told these niggaz that D-Block sent them after them?"

"I doubt it," Maine answered. "Take into account how long it's been. And them niggaz from Harrisburg ain't made a move yet. I really don't think they took Diane seriously," Maine concluded, which they both knew would be a grave mistake on their behalf. Only a fool, or someone who didn't know Diane, would think that she didn't mean something she said.

"From where I'm sitting," Thugg said. "I don't think it's a situation where they don't believe her. And I could be wrong.

But I think this so-called Don Angelino may be thinking he can out-smart her."

It wasn't the first time he'd had the thought. Thugg had been thinking that for a while.

The average nigga in the game didn't think that a female could hold a candle to them. They certainly never met a woman like D-Block. So for someone like this Don Angelino to meet her based on everything others said about her, there was a more than 50% chance that he thought there was more hype than reality.

"So you think Angelino's going to be stupid and try her gangster?" Maine asked.

Thugg sighed before he spoke his next words. "Look," Thugg said. "She's your partner. Me, I met her through you, bruh. So ya know more about her than I do. I'm just calling things the way I see them. From a street nigga point of view, a nigga in power ain't gone bow down to a female that ain't prove herself, in his eyes. Fuck what everybody else say about her."

Maine thought about what he said. While it was a harsh reality, he too could see the point in what Thugg just explained. Now he was wondering if Diane had given it that much thought as well.

**

Burner didn't even question it when Nico sent the text. She'd said that because he was really helping her out, she wanted to treat him and his boys to a night out with her and some of her girlfriends. When he mentioned it to One Blood, it seemed that he and the rest of his litter were down.

"Yo, Sun, how these bitches be looking down here?" One Blood asked.

He was riding in the Tahoe with Burner, while his crew followed them in the Land Rover. They were on their way to this club Magic City.

"Shit. The lil bitch I'm fuckin' with is too fine. Plus, I know she be wit' another lil bad bitch. I doubt she fucks wit any bitches that ain't on the same level they on," Burner explained.

"Nigga, say word." One Blood gave a big smile.

"Bruh, I'm telling you," Burner reiterated.

He even pulled out a sack of cocaine, which had the little spoon inside. Coming to a stop at a red light, Burner opened it and used the spoon to serve up both nostrils. Then, while the light was still red, he passed it to One Blood. The younger man followed his example and also served each nostril. Then he handed it back.

"Yeah, bro. I can't wait to fuck some of this county pussy. Niggaz been looking forward to some shit like this since we arrived," One Blood added.

Not long after that they pulled into the Club's parking lot, all of them got out and followed Burner as he led the way. Once inside, he pulled his phone out and texted Nico. He waited, and the text that came back said something about one of her girls was still getting ready. So Burner led them to a couple of tables.

The only thing they could do was get a few drinks and wait, so they ordered Patron, and Hennessy Black. They broke out the cocaine again and started the party anyway. Besides, there were more than enough bitches up in the club that were single.

***

In the movies, it was usually just called C-4 plastic explosives, but the technical term was semtex. The killer had never used it before. But when he got it, the people he got it from did explain to him how to use it. In fact, as he crept through the parking lot in all black clothing, finding his way to the two trucks, without being seen, he knew that it wouldn't be that hard to set the two packages. He dropped to his back and crawled under the Tahoe. The killer attached the packages to the gas tank, and made sure that it wouldn't come loose. He then flipped a switch, and a green light came on. The package was now live. In his pocket, he had the detonator. All he had to do now was secure the next package to the Land Rover. After that, it would come down to a waiting game.

He could have taken them all out one by one, but time was of the essence. This way, he would be able to get them all. So, he didn't have anything else to do tonight. The killer finished what he was doing, and then crawled from under the trucks. Once he was sure he'd been unseen by anyone who might have been close by, he then faded into the night.

***

"Ayo, Sun. Ain't that the nigga, Burner, wit' them red niggaz?" Justice asked.

He and Damian had been inside of their private VIP booth, drinking and smoking blunts. The last thing they expected to see was this nigga, Burner, showing up with six more bloody niggaz. After Jersey got killed, they hadn't seen too much of Burner around. Justice watched as Damian squinted his eyes, trying to get a clear look out of the window.

"Yeah, yeah, I think that is the nigga. But I don't know who them other niggaz is, though," Damian stated.

Thug Life 3

They both sat there silently for a while, in their own thoughts.

"Ayo, you think that nigga got still got ill thoughts towards wifey?" Damian asked.

"Maybe," Justice declared. Then he fell quietly in thought for a few minutes. Justice brought his drink up and took a good swallow of it. Then he spoke. "We probably should go ahead and whack this nigga, gon' head and get it over wit before he builds his nuts up again," Justice said.

Damian didn't respond immediately. Instead, it seemed he was thinking it over.

"You think wifey gone be mad after we murk this nigga?" Damian asked.

By the way he asked, Justice knew that they were going to kill Burner.

"What?" Justice twisted his face up. "Yo, Sun. Let a nigga find out. Let a nigga find out you worried about wifey being mad. Yo, I swear, I'ma let niggaz back home know."

He was still talking. Damian, on the other hand, leaned forward and grabbed one of the blunts off the table in front of them. He put fire to the end of it, and took a few tokes.

"Ayo, you wanna hit this?" Damian asked. "Sun. Don't play, Sun. Yo, pass the fuckin' blunt. Nigga, pass the Dutch, nigga," Justice said.

Damian handed him the blunt. Then he lifted his glass and sipped his drink.

"Yo. You gotta let sis know you ain't coming home tonight?" Damian asked, referring to Juanita. She and Justice had something serious going on now. He watched as Justice passed the blunt back after he'd hit it several times.

"You know what, Sun?" Justice asked.

"Nah, what, God?" Damian said.

"Yo. I think I'm about to wife shorty. Gone head and get it over wit," Justice stated.

Damian paused halfway with the blunt to his lips and looked over at him. He twisted his face.

"You, Sun?" Damian began. "Let a nigga find out you on some old cuddle up type shit. Let a nigga find out.

He then hit the blunt several times. Now it was at the half-way mark. Damian paused and asked. "So we gon' dead these niggaz tonight?"

Justice tilted his head in thought. "More like in the morning, Sun," he answered.

They both fell silent after that, and polished off the blunt together.

***

Burner had to hold One Blood up as they stumbled out of the club. The punk ass bitch, Nico, hadn't shown up. That kind of made it look like he'd been flexing to these niggaz. They'd even made some jokes about him not really having a bad bitch on his hip. He'd spent most of the night texting back and forth with her, and the bitch wouldn't even send him a photo. She claimed one of her girls had gotten sick, said something about her having food poison or some shit.

He didn't know how true that was. Either way, they'd snorted up the rest of the coke and drank enough Don Q and William Selyem to put a bull to sleep. Burner was really tripping, though, because these young gunners couldn't handle their liquor. All six of them were fucked up. It would be a wonder if they could make it back to the motel, especially seeing how they were all trying to make it across the parking lot.

They made it, and somehow managed to get inside of the trucks. Burner, once again, had One Blood with him, while the

other 5 were in the Land Rover they'd driven down in. He
started the Tahoe and waited while they started the Rover.
Then he pulled out first. Burner managed to reach the entrance
to the parking lot, which led back out to the street. He waited
while the Rover caught up and nearly clipped his bumper.

***

Both Damian and Justice followed the niggaz outside. For
them, it wasn't an issue making it to Justice's black Escalade.
However, when they got inside and Justice started the truck,
they waited, wanting to put some distance between them and
the two trucks.

"Yo, Sun. Where ya want it to go down at?" Justice asked.

While Damian was thinking, they watched as the Land
Rover nearly rammed the Tahoe from behind. But it didn't.
And just as Damian was about to speak, the entire night lit up.

The two explosions seemed like one large explosion. They
were both so big that it lit the whole parking lot up and shook
all of the other cars that were parked. Most of the car alarms
came on, due to the force of the winds that rocked them. As
the light grew dim, both Justice and Damian's eyesight began
to clear.

When they looked, they could see that there wasn't much
left of the two trucks.

"Yooo, Sun," Justice glanced over at Damian.

"The fuck you do when you went to the bathroom and
shit? Nigga, ya was gone like twenty minutes and shit," Justice stated.

But Damian said, "I didn't do that."

Justice looked disbelievingly at him. "What? Nigga, say
word," Justice said.

Damian just shook his head. Then he looked out the windshield and watched the trucks burn.

***

The killer sat there and watched as the two New York dudes sat in the Escalade. He knew who they were, just like he knew they were both watching the two trucks burn. But it didn't really matter. He'd done what he was sent to do. Now all he had to do was wait for the next call. His job still wasn't over. He'd been told that the last body to fall would be the hardest one to drop. But he didn't put that much thought into it. One thing he knew for sure, if a nigga could die, if he could stop breathing, then he would eventually find a way to make him rest in peace.

Chapter Seventeen
Four Weeks Later...

Damian sat on the couch playing *Need for Speed* on his PlayStation. He was all into the game when Diane entered the den. He saw her out of the corner of his eye. But didn't make any sudden moves to let her know that he saw her. Then she moved so that she was standing in his direct eyesight. Damian noticed that she was looking down at him with a scowl on her face. He'd told himself over the past four weeks that he wasn't going to get pulled into her game.

"Yo, I don't know why you mean muggin' me and shit," Damian stated. "I already told you. Me and Sun didn't have anything to do with them niggaz getting murked."

"Mhm. Whatever, nigga," Diane said.

She then rolled her head on her shoulder and sucked her teeth as she turned and left. Damian still didn't understand all of that. He would have thought that she'd be glad some of her enemies had been killed. But instead, she threw a fit because she claimed him and Justice were running around Augusta killing everybody. And she didn't believe neither one of them when they tried to tell her they didn't kill Jersey nor Burner and them young niggaz with him. Yet she didn't believe it.

"Whatever my ass," Damian said under his breath. Since he was the only one in the room, he knew that only he could hear his words.

"If I wanted to kill a nigga, I would just fuckin' kill the nigga. I ain't gotta lie about that shit," he mumbled.

"You do know I can muthfuckin' hear you down this hall-way right?" Diane called out.

He nearly jumped, thinking she was close to him, when she wasn't.

"Yeah. Whatever," he threw back at her.

"Nigga, don't play wit me," she hollered back. But Damian was already moving on to his next thoughts.

Just the other day, Maine had pulled him aside and said he was worried. He'd said something about Diane underestimating this nigga Don Angelino. The nigga still hadn't made good on the proposition she'd made for them to do something about the twins. And the shit was just now starting to get to him. Now he was wondering if she really was slipping or something. He didn't want to get into her business by asking questions. That just wasn't how their relationship was built.

With a sigh, he decided to let it go. There really wasn't much he could do about it. But then he did think about one thing, and it just might work. The first thing he needed to do, though, was have a word with these people, see what they had to say about the situation.

***

When Juanita pulled into the parking lot, she drove the dark grey Mercedes-Benz SL-Class convertible like it should have been a race car. But when she stepped out of the car, she didn't look anything like Danica Patrick, rocking her Jimmy Choo's and Ferragamo khaki pants with a Fendi blouse. She also carried her $1,200 Gucci imported purse like she was carrying P.J. Morgan's bank on her shoulder. So when she pulled the door open and stepped into the main body of the Augusta mall, she entered like she owned the place.

Juanita really couldn't believe it when Justice came into the house and handed her the pre-paid credit card. Then he told her to go treat herself. She assumed it only held a little bit of money, until she called the customer service number and was told that the card held six thousand dollars.

When she stepped inside of the spa, she smiled at her old friend.

"Juanita. It's so nice to have you back with us," the white woman said as she met her at the door. "Thank you, Lita. It's so nice to be back," Juanita said.

She'd known when she made the appointment that the woman would meet her. Lita was the manager of the spa. Back when Juanita first came to Augusta, she'd spent quite a bit of time getting spa treatments. Back then, her brother ran the business, and she didn't have to.

That was, up until he started making poor decisions and playing around with Young Castro's people.

"Please, come this way. I have everything all set up for you," Lita explained.

She led Juanita into the prep room and left her with the girls, who were waiting for her there.

The Hispanic Community had a good thing going on in the Central Ave area. They pretty much had control of the entire area. While there were still quite a bit of older blacks living in the area, there were never any problems between the blacks and Hispanics. That was until her brother started trying to turn Dogg.

Hernandez had actually tricked Dogg with his lust for the material lifestyle. When Dogg met Gloria and started hanging around Central Ave, he was seeing all of the flexing Hernandez and his boys were doing, and he wanted that lifestyle. So Hernandez was able to convince him to betray Young Castro, which was the worst mistake he had ever made. Now Dogg, Hernandez, and his soldiers were all dead. Dead by the hands of Young Castro.

Juanita lay upon the table face down, while the two younger women gave her a full body massage. Her mind kept thinking over how far she'd come since the days of her brother. Now there were more Hispanics, Latin Americans, Puerto Ricans and Chicano's throughout Augusta. They were everywhere, and they all worked for her.

Juanita was actually the Mexican version of what Diane was to the streets. And since she'd moved more Hispanics in, Diane was giving her enough product to keep them all under control. In essence, they also worked for Diane. They just didn't know it.

The reason the thought even came to her was because Diane had asked for the use of Juanita's Sicario hit squad, whom she would be meeting with later that night. Juanita would explain to them that these people in Lake Almstead and Harrisburg were in violation, and that they were trying to make it hard for them to make money. With the amount of money the Hispanics were making under her, she knew they weren't going to let anybody stop that. So they had to help protect their investment.

Diane didn't want them to do all of the work. She'd just told Juanita that she needed her people as back up. The real work would be done by her Street Sweepers, which meant that all her Sicario had to do was seal off both areas so that no one got away. This seemed easy enough. She'd be explaining all of that when she met with her people later. Juanita just didn't know yet when Diane planned to make her move. As long as she'd known the other woman, she knew it was a pretty strong chance they wouldn't know until it was time to move.

***

Alicia gave Thugg the evil eye as she got up from the bed. Naked, she walked to the bathroom, while Thugg sat up with his back to the headboard, watching. The damn girl was just beautiful. This being only the second time they'd come together sexually, Thugg had to go ahead and admit it to himself. The damn girl had him fucked up. He liked everything about her, everything except the fact that she was about to become one of the Street Sweepers.

Thugg wasn't against women who could kill. Everybody knew that D-Block was one of the best that ever did it. He just never thought that he would have a woman that would stand beside him during an actual gun battle. He didn't know how he would react if something went wrong and she got hit. He'd tried to talk her out of it last night, but the woman was just too stubborn and headstrong. She claimed that she'd been doing this when she was in Florida, and that down there some of the neighborhoods were rougher than what she'd seen in Augusta. Thugg didn't doubt that. After all, he had robbed a few niggaz in Florida a few years back.

Thugg sighed as he heard her flush the toilet. Yeah, it was something he had to deal with. The life of a thug wasn't strictly male, women also had a right to it.

***

Maine watched as Imani still moped as she moved about the house. She was still mourning the death of her friend, and it was four weeks and a funeral later. The police said that she'd been dead inside of her SUV for at least a day before someone found her. There were no fingerprints, and the only thing missing was her phone, which they'd found the day after they found the body. It was in a dumpster behind a restaurant in North Augusta. They'd found texts of an arranged meeting with some guy. The guy wasn't found until autopsies of the bodies pulled from the explosion at Club Magic City came in.

Dental records confirmed that one of those guys was the one Nico had been texting.

Maine brushed it off. He really didn't have time for all of that. Diane had all of them on high alert and stand-by, so they were all waiting to receive the word. If they didn't know nothing else, they knew that something was about to go down soon. And it wouldn't be pretty.

***

"So you don't have anything?" Imani whispered as she spoke into the phone.

She was hiding in the bedroom, secretly making the call. Lord forbid Maine ever found out about it.

"Not anything solid," Officer Jackson said. "I've looked into the possibility of her having your friend and these people in the club parking lot killed, and so far, nothing leads back to her. The strongest thing we have on this woman is her possible organized crime dealings," he explained.

She sighed. "Okay, so you do have something on her. You'll still be able to arrest her," Imani said.

On the other end of the phone, GBI Officer Anthony Jackson was sitting at a desk. Lying on the desk before him was a partial service record. Apparently, Diane Blaylock had been a Navy Seal, which wouldn't be strange, except for all of the redacted portions of the file. Then there was a part that was simply missing. All he had was her entrance in the Navy, and then four years were missing. It started back right before she left service.

In his experience, Jackson knew there was only one thing that explained something like that, Special Ops work.

"I'm not so sure about that just yet," he said into the phone, while still looking at the file before him. "Just give me some more time. I think I'll be able to build a case."

He ended the call, and then sat back in his chair. Although he'd said that, his mind was telling him something different. He was no longer confident in his ability to bring this woman down, especially since his lieutenant wasn't making an effort to assist. Something about that didn't smell right. Jackson shook his head, he just didn't know.

Trai'Quan

Chapter Eighteen

"As you both know," Angelino began as he looked at both of the men that sat before him, one being his uncle, and the other his second in command.

"Because of that job we pulled a few months ago, we've found ourselves in an unusual position. This woman, D-Block, has given me a choice. It's either I do something about the two guys who gave me the information, or we suffer the same punishment as they do," he outlined.

"And this said punishment is what, death?" Black Money asked.

"Pretty much," Angelino continued. "She made it my responsibility to kill these guys for their so-called disrespect. Now, in theory, she has a logical point. When I sent you out to do the job, I wasn't given fore knowledge as to *who* the targets were. So we were in the blind."

Silence followed for a moment as they all sat there and contemplated the words.

"Ok. So these niggaz with the information were in the wrong," Black Money vented. "Then we go clip these niggaz and everybody is happy. Unless she's asking for the product back, because it's too late for all of that."

Angelino pretty much knew that giving the product back wasn't an option. He hadn't even given that part of it any real thought because she never mentioned it.

"No. She's not asking for the product back," he stated, now wondering why that really was.

Black Money realized that he was the one doing all of the talking. He glanced over to where Teflon sat quietly. And Teflon simply hunched his shoulders.

"So what seems to be the problem then?" Black Money looked back and forth between both Angelino and Teflon. He was confused. The most logical thing to do would be to keep the peace with these people, especially considering they had access to so much product.

"The problem is," Angelino began. "While I do respect D-Block as a business person, I do not respect her as a bitch telling a Don what he *will* do."

He'd slightly raised his voice when he said the last part. He wanted to emphasize the parts that defined what power was.

"Look." Angelino calmed himself. "This isn't about pride. So try to see it from a position of what would come next. If I take the threat, and we kill these guys, it won't hurt us. But let's say something comes up between us and D-Block's people later. She'll expect us to bow down, be it right or wrong. If we concede power to her now, it'll bite us in the ass later," he explained. When he finished, he look closely at both of them.

Still and yet it was Black Money who spoke. "So, we're going to war with these muthafuckaz?" he questioned.

"Not necessarily," Angelino stated calmly. "You see, if she goes after the twins first, it'll most likely weaken her defenses. From what I've been told, these guys have brought in some more people from Atlanta. And I think they're targeting D-Block directly," he explained.

What he wasn't telling them was that he'd set into motion for information to reach the twins. The said information would, if they went for it, push the twins to openly attack D-Block or her people. That, in turn, would have a chain reaction, and cause the two of them to do whatever. If she killed the twins, hopefully she'd lose some people. And if the twins killed her, then his overall problem was solved. But he kept that little information to himself.

***

"MOB shit," Micky called out as he stepped out of his ride and approached the other man.

They were meeting this time in the parking lot of Chuck E. Cheese. Micky had said that he couldn't be seen meeting up with either Leroy or his brother. Leroy, on the other hand, was leaning back on to his SUV, waiting.

"Whoa," He responded to the call that his fellow mob member made.

They shook hands, once Micky reached him. It had been his idea to park on the other side of the parking lot, and not close to Leroy's Chevy Blazer.

"Shawty, I got your message. So what's going on, Shawty?" Leroy asked.

"Shawty," Micky began. "They coming for you, Shawty. That bitch and her lil crew, they getting ready to pull up on your scene, Shawty," Micky said.

He'd been ear hustling and listening in on as many of Don Angelino's private conversations as he could. So when he got wind of D-Block pulling all of her people together to make a major move on Lake Almstead, he quickly sent a text to Leroy that they needed to meet ASAP.

"Shawty. We got some more MOB niggaz with us now, Shawty. Twin went back home and got us some back up. So we might be good, Shawty," Leroy told him.

"I hear you, Shawty. But, Shawty, is you willing to go up against this bitch with just a few niggaz? Shawty, the bitch got an army, Shawty," Micky said.

He watched as Leroy considered what he said. Micky knew all too well from the information that Don Angelino gathered on D-Block that everything they assumed was hype, really wasn't. And then there was the niggaz she had in her crew.

"I think we can handle it, Shawty," Leroy told him, and even sounded like he believed it. "Shawty, we gon' ride with these killas we got on our team, Shawty." Leroy nodded and gave him a smile all at once.

Micky stood there and looked at him funny-like for a second. Then, after coming to a conclusion, he pat Leroy on the back. "Alright, Shawty. I need to get back before someone notices I'm not around, Shawty. But, Shawty, y'all niggaz be careful, Shawty." Micky fist bumped with him. Then he turned and walked back to his own ride.

There wasn't anything else that he could do. If these niggaz thought that they were ready for what this bitch was about, then so be it. He'd done what he was supposed to do.

***

Lil Zay sat inside of his Ford F-150, parked at a gas station. He was parked over next to the pay phones. He was talking on his cell phone. The whole time that he sat there, though, he had his eyes on Micky, watching him talking to this twin nigga.

When Don Angelino first told him to keep an eye on this nigga, he wasn't exactly sure why. Then he'd followed the nigga to that so-called secret meeting in Penalton King Park. That was when he first saw the nigga meeting the twin. He didn't know *what* they were talking about. But he did know Angelino suspected him of some type of bullshit.

Now here the nigga was meeting this twin again. Lil Zay knew something was going on, he just couldn't say what it was. But he had an idea Don Angelino knew far more than what he was telling anyone. Yet then again, that wasn't his job to worry about what Don Angelino had going on. He was just doing what he was told. Anything else was uncivilized.

***

Don Angelino smiled as he looked out the window. He'd ended the call only seconds ago. But he was in a good mood, knowing that everything was going as planned. He'd found out quite a while ago that it was Micky who'd turned these niggaz on to him. At first, he wondered how this nigga Leroy knew to come to him with information of a good robbery. So he'd personally set out a whole week where he dressed in all black, stole a hot box, and watched these twins as they did their business.

On the 4th day, this nigga, Micky, showed up. He'd even been moving like he was up to something. But once Angelino made the connection, he knew what to look for. He later found out that Micky was also from the 'A' but niggaz in Augusta accepted him into the folds because he had family in Augusta. Yet, Angelino knew where his heart was, so he'd begun to feed him bad information. And sure enough, this fool passed it along. That was right along with what Don Angelino had planned.

Trai'Quan

Chapter Nineteen

"Okay. Let's get this money."

Diane looked around at everyone that was there. They were at the darkest part of the parking lot of the VA hospital on Laney Walker Blvd. She looked first at Juanita, who stood next to the dark blue Chevrolet Suburban. Along with her were four other Mexicans, and they never spoke, so nobody knew their names. And nobody intended to ask. Then there was Maine and Thugg. They too stood next to a dark Suburban. Justice stood with Damian next to the black Suburban he and Diane would be riding in.

"The niggaz in Lake Almstead been adding on to their numbers, and we don't know if they're dangerous or not." Diane looked over to where Maine and Thugg stood. "I need you two to take care of that for me. We gon' let y'all get started ten minutes before we move. Juanita and her team are going to back you up. But I need you two to do the work. Can y'all handle that?"

Diane rolled her eyes, and then turned her attention to Damian and Justice, who seemed to be patiently waiting. "I need you two to rush up into these Loe Life Mafia niggaz spot. Dead as many niggaz as you can. There's a green light on any and everybody in that area. Am I making myself clear?" she asked.

"Wait a minute. Wait a minute," Justice said as he glanced around. "You mean, you're giving *us* the green light to dead any nigga in Harrisburg? I mean, any nigga?" he asked.

"Yeah, smart ass." Diane smirked. "Any nigga, except this so-called Don. That nigga belongs to me."

"Wait a minute. Wait a minute," Damian said as he mimicked Justice. "So you and Alicia gon' be *our* back?" he asked.

Trai'Quan

This time Diane threw up her hands, frustrated. Then she sighed. "Are you niggaz through yet? I kinda wanna get back home to my babies," Diane stated.

As she stood there mean-mugging both Justice and Damian, everyone else shook their heads like they couldn't believe what they were seeing.

Damian looked at Justice, and then Justice looked at him. Then they turned to face her.

"Ok. Okay." They both reached under their waists and pulled out two guns apiece. "Let's go kill some niggaz," Damian said.

Everyone started getting into their Suburbans.

***

The First Ten Minutes

"Okay, Shawty," Leroy said as he looked around at this team. "Shawty, the word is this bitch gon' pull up, Shawty. And they saying the bitch got an army. So we gon' have to be on point, Shawty."

They were all outfitted with an assortment of guns, having already known everything was leading up to this moment.

"Caesar, I need you and Juge down on this end of the street." Leroy pointed. "Y'all gon' be with me, while Marcus and Monte' gone be with T-Roy down on that end," he added, pointing towards the back of Lake Almstead.

He waited while their soldiers moved out. Then he turned to his twin. "What's on your mind, Shawty?" Leroy asked.

He watched as his twin hunched his shoulders. "I don't know, Shawty," T-Roy said, causing Leroy to look at him with uncertainty.

136

After all, T-Roy was the reason they were even going through all of this. Had he been willing to listen and compromise, just a little, they wouldn't be going to war with some people they really didn't know all too well.

"Shawty," T-Roy began. "Shawty, I'm thinking that I might have been wrong, Shawty. I'm thinking that maybe we shouldn't have made that move, Shawty. I mean, we split the shit with them Loe Life Mafia niggaz. But where they at, Shawty?" T-Roy asked, as if he were about to cry.

The whole time, Leroy stood there looking at him with a sad expression upon his face. This was his flesh and blood, the exact same copy as he was.

"Look, Shawty. We already here now. It's too late to go back. So you gon' have to suck that shit up, Shawty, and get yo head back in the game," Leroy explained to him.

He watched as his twin thought his words over with a contemplative expression on his face. Then T-Roy nodded and stood up straight, with his chest poked out.

Leroy knew then that his brother was back. And he smiled on the inside.

***

They split up before they reached Lake Almstead. Thugg took it upon himself to walk straight up Broad Street, while Maine went around by where the Boy's Club used to be. He was the first one to reach his destination.

When he came closer, Maine saw the three men standing around with their guns out. Off the top, they looked tough. But at the end of the day, you were only as tough as your heart would allow you to be. If it wasn't in your heart, then it wasn't in you. Some niggaz were just pussy, trying their best to avoid hard dicks.

Maine knew this, which was why when he looked at the niggaz who stood before him, he'd already counted them dead. All he had to do now was make it happen. He ducked down behind, or on the side of, a Lincoln MKS sedan, and then pulled out his two Glock .40's and checked the clips. He needed to get the first few shots off first because from where he crouched, he could see these niggaz had AR-15's Uzi's. He couldn't see what one of them had, but it looked like a shotgun, maybe even a pump. He wasn't trying to get hit with either of those, if he could avoid it.

***

Thugg didn't even wait that long. As he came a breast of the top of the hill, he saw one of the twins. He didn't know one of the other niggaz, but he did recognized one of them. He was the second nigga that he'd robbed that time in Atlanta. Thugg reached under his trench coat and brought out his baby. The Ithaca Mag 10 was an extremely powerful shotgun. It was as strong as the guns used to bring down elephants. So powerful was it that the standard gun only came with three shots. Thugg took his to someone and had it modified, so now it held two extra shots. When he brought the gun up and squeezed the trigger, it sounded like Jesus was talking.

Boom.

Juge didn't even know that he was dead. The round that went into his left shoulder tore everything away, shoulder, upper torso, and part of his neck.

"Oh shit, Shawty. Oh shit. Nigga, run," Caesar called out as they both saw Juge's body go down.

Leroy dropped to the ground behind a red pickup truck, just as the next round tore into it. The damage done by the round was excoriating. It wouldn't just remove outer flesh, it tore into the truck as if it was flesh and blood.

"What the fuck is that nigga shooting?" Leroy rolled over and came up squeezing.

He was using a Taurus .45, so his shots were also kind of loud. Not as loud as the shotgun, but they were heard.

***

"Oh, shit, Shawty," Marcus exclaimed. He turned and looked up towards the top of the hill where the sound of the shotgun came from.

"What the fuck is that?" Monte' asked.

But before either one could decide to go check, Maine came up from behind the Lincoln, both guns spitting flames.

Boca. Boca. Boca.

It seemed like there was an echo with each shot.

The first of his bullets to make real contact entered T-Roy's face just under his right eye, along with two more, one to the neck and one to the chest, center mass. He was dead before anyone got off their first shot. But even as T-Roy went down, an exchange of fire began. Now it seemed like bullets were flying everywhere.

Whoever squeezed the trigger on the Uzi didn't know how to let go. Maine watched the fire spit from the gun as it swung in his direction. But just as he was about to duck behind the Lincoln again, Maine heard the AR-15 come to life, and felt his body being hit a number of times.

He spun to his right and squeezed off another series of shots. However, being hit by the AR-15 was quickly becoming an issue for him. Maine didn't know how bad the hits were. All he knew was that he was losing his grip on his gun.

His body went down just as he completed the turn with his whole body.

"I think I got 'im, Shawty," Monte called out, while Marcus was removing the clip from the Uzi and pushing in another one.

"Come on, Shawty, let's go pop this nigga," Marcus said.

They spread out, making a harder target as they moved towards where they'd seen Maine go down on the other side of the car. It didn't take them long to find him, especially with the blood pouring out of the holes.

Maine was slipping in and out of consciousness as he tried to roll over. But it seemed like his body wasn't obeying his commands. His vision was blurry, but he did see the pair of legs that came to a stop over him.

"Gon' head and kill Shawty." He heard one of them say.

Marcus aimed downward and squeezed. With the Uzi being automatic, and having a filed down firing pin, it cut loose extremely fast, damn near sending the whole clip into Maine's body.

"That's what I'm talking about, Shawty," Monte' said as he looked at the other man. "Now let's go see if we-"

"Damn shame what you vatos just did to that thug."

Both Marcus and Monte' turned to see the two Mexicans who'd seemed to materialize out of thin air or something.

"Listen, Shawty. Why don't you amigos gon' bout y'all business, Shawty? Shawty, this ain't got nothing to do wit y'all, Shawty," Marcus said.

They both watched as the two Mexicans smiled. Then they reached under their shirts and withdrew two pistols. At first, Monte' and Marcus were confused. They didn't have beef with any Mexicans.

"Unfortunately, homes," one of the Mexicans smiled at them as he raised his gun. "This is Thug Life homie. And you just killed one of ours."

Neither Marcus nor Monte' could react quickly enough as the Mexican unloaded his clip into both of them. When they were done, they looked down at the fallen soldier.

"D-Block ain't gone like this, homes," one said.

"I know, vato. But shiiit, wasn't nothing we could do to save him," the other said.

***

Thugg looked down into Leroy's face as he stood over him. He'd already put him down, and had just delivered the last slug from his Desert Eagle. Leroy was dead, along with the other two who'd been with him. Thugg turned as he heard a whistle somewhere behind him

"What's up?" one of the Mexicans asked.

"Just finishing up," Thugg told them. "What's up with everything down the hill?"

"Oh, homes," the other one spoke. "Your friend, he didn't make it."

Thugg paused for a minute as he looked at them. But then reality kicked in.

"A'ight. Let's go see if they need some help down in Harrisburg," Thugg stated.

There was no sense crying over spilled milk. Maine was gone, and he wasn't coming back. It would be Diane who took the news the hardest. She was the whole reason that they were even a part of the Street Sweepers.

Trai'Quan

Chapter Twenty

As soon as they set foot outside of the stolen car, both Damian and Justice pulled their guns and started shooting any and everybody they saw that looked like they were dope dealers. To the dope boys throughout Harrisburg, it seemed like they were under fire by twenty shooters. Too busy running, no one thought to look and see who exactly was doing the shooting. They just assumed that there were more than two men. What really gave off the impression of there being more than two shooters was that Damian held two FN Five Sevens, both of which carried twenty 5.7 x 28 mm armor-piercing rounds. And the expansion speed could be changed. Damian started out shooting single shots, then switched to semi-automatic.

Justice favored his twin FNS-9's, which were polymer framed. They fired 9mm rounds, with a four-inch hammer-forged barrel and polished feed ramp. Both guns were fully ambidextrous and had loading chamber indicators. They had crisp audible-resetting triggers and seventeen-round magazines.

With that type of precision from four guns, and bodies falling all around, it was easy to assume there were several shooters.

***

Sitting inside of the black Nissan Armada parked further back, next to the curve, Diane and Alicia watched as the magic unfolded before them.

"Dese Street Sweepers yu got, dey really good," Alicia stated.

"Dese niggaz just get on my last nerve, though," Diane stated, and the younger woman laughed.

Diane had never had the opportunity to watch either Damian or Justice in their natural element. But as they now sat watching, she realized that they were both the epitome of killing. She'd been trained to kill, but at that moment, she was impressed beyond all measure. They watched as one nigga tried to run out from the side of a house and attack Damian, only to have him turn and slap the nigga with one of his guns. Damian lifted his left foot and kicked him, then step forward and pushed the gun barrel into his chest and squeezed.

"Dat one de rim yo'r man. I'm real good at dis," Alicia said.

They watched as Damian continued walking up the street with Justice, two killing machines. Diane couldn't even say anything. All she could do was sit there and shake her head. What Alicia didn't know (she didn't think), was that both of them were so high it didn't make sense. She still couldn't see how they did all this killing and was high.

***

"Come on, nephew. We've got to get you out of here," Teflon said as he burst into the room.

Angelino was standing at the window, looking out into the streets. He was seeing all of his people out there dying, and there was nothing that he could do to save them.

"It's all my fault," Angelino nearly whispered.

"We ain't got time for all of that, nephew. I've just gotten off the phone with your old man. The family has the jet on the way to Hartsfield/Jackson airport. It'll be there by the time we get there," Teflon stated.

He sighed with relief when he saw Angelino begin moving. He knew he would have a hard time explaining to one of the Italian Mafia's Under Bosses why his son was killed.

Angelino's old man started out as a hitter for the bosses. Even with his weakness for dark flesh, he still managed to move up the ladder. But Angelino wasn't accepted into the pure blood family in New York. They were aware of him, and he was under their protection. But at the end of the day, he was just another bastard child by one of the pure bloods.

The only reason they were sending the private jet down was because Angelino was a good investment. When money was made, Angelino would be sure to send twenty percent back to his old man's Don. And in return, they would help him out whenever they could.

It didn't take long for them to pack his bags. Most of them were on stand-by in case something like this ever happened, a contingency plan of sorts.

"We should have just took those twins out," Angelino mumbled to himself. "It was just that simple."

Teflon shook his head as they walked through the house. Black Money was waiting with the Range Rover outside. It was an hour's drive to Atlanta, taking I-20, a straight shot. All they had to do was make it out of Harrisburg alive.

They exited the front of the house, with Teflon leading the way. Everything looked safe, all the way to the Range. Black Money stood just outside of the driver's door, holding a MP5K, which was a short H&K sub-machine gun that was designed in the early 1970's. They'd just reached the truck and Teflon was about to open the back door when Micky appeared out of nowhere.

"Boss. These muthafuckaz are everywhere. What do you want me to do?" Micky's eye looked to the Range Rover, and then to Teflon.

But it was Angelino who spoke. "Is everybody dead?" he asked.

"Nah, I don't think everybody is," Micky said. "From the looks of it, we might have a trader on the inside." Micky added.

But he didn't see the way that Angelino looked at him. Nor did he see the Don pull out his gun. The Beretta 9 mm wasn't all that big, not compared to all of the bigger guns being used in the streets.

Micky turned back to face him. When he saw the gun pointed at him, his eyes widened.

"We knew you were sleeping with the enemy," Angelino said as he squeezed the trigger.

As Micky's body fell to the sidewalk, Teflon opened the back door of the Range Rover and let Angelino climb inside. He then climbed in behind him. Once they were in, Black Money got in and started the truck. Then he pulled away.

***

Her cell phone rang and nearly startled her. Diane pulled it out and saw it was Damian.

"Yeah," she answered.

"There's a black Range coming your way, ma. Inside is the Don, and his two Lieutenants," Damian said.

"Alright. You two mop this shit up. I want every swinging dick that don't work for me dead. Me and my girl got these niggaz," she stressed.

No sooner had she said that than the Range Rover flew by them.

"Hey." She snapped her fingers. "That's them. Follow at a good distance."

Alicia started the Armada and got behind the Range. She made it a point not to get close. So she kept a block's distance between them, just enough so that she could still see them.

"Where the fuck are they going?" Diane said to herself as Alicia drove.

Alicia hunched her shoulders. She had no idea. She was just following orders. And she couldn't wait for her chance to kill.

***

Damian walked over to where Justice sat on the top steps of the house's porch. Both of his guns lay on the step next to him, and he was rolling up the weed in a vanilla flavored paper.

"You know, Sun," Justice said as he licked the paper and pressed it together. "I been thinking 'bout taking wifey on a vacation or something."

"Oh, so now it's wifey, huh?" Damian said.

But Justice acted like he didn't hear him and kept talking as he dug into his pocket for a light. "I'm thinking some ole cruise ship shit. You know." He paused to light the blunt. Then he took a few hits off it.

"Yeah. I'm thinking, you and sis might need a getaway, too. You know." Justice held the blunt out to him.

As it stood, they'd gunned down just about everything in Harrisburg. And they could just now hear the police sirens in the distance.

"You think we got 'em all?" Damian asked.

But before Justice could answer, they looked up and saw the Chevy Blazer pull up.

"Yo. You niggaz gone wait on the cops, or do you need a ride?" Thugg asked.

It didn't take them long to hop in and for him to pull out of Harrisburg.

"Yo, what happened to your manz and them?" Damien asked. He knew all too well that Maine was the one who brought Thugg into the fold.

"He didn't make it," Thugg stated.

He drove for a minute in silence. All of them seemed to be thinking along the same lines.

"Yo, wifey gon' flip when she hear that," Damian stated.

Diane didn't have too many best friends, and Maine had been just that for her. They went all the way back to grade school. Now they were going to have to tell her that he became a casualty of this little war.

***

GBI agent Jackson Anthony was one of the first on the scene, which wasn't unusual. They had a file on many of those killed throughout Harrisburg and Lake Almstead tonight. Jackson walked through the crime scene and looked at the bodies. From the way it looked, somebody had a serious issue with the Loe Life Mafia, and these twins. And it looked like all of the fatalities were the locals.

"Boy, whoever they pissed off was serious," one of the investigators said.

"What makes you say that?" Jackson asked.

He watched as the detective squatted next to one of the bodies and pulled the sheet back.

"You see this right here?" He pointed to the body at certain areas. "Whatever the perpetrator was shooting, it was just short of a fucking cannon, something like a baby bazooka. We won't know for sure what it was until the autopsy. But I'm telling you, these people were serious."

Jackson could clearly see that whatever was used, it seemed to have obliterated the upper portion of the body. There was barely enough of the head left to identify.

"Agent Anthony. Over here," one of his agents called to him.

When he walked over and saw what it was, the pieces suddenly began to fall into place.

"This guy wasn't one of them. We've got him in on some other cases," the agent said.

Jackson already knew who the guy was. When Imani came to him, he'd made it a point to do a complete background check on her. So he knew that this guy was her baby's father. The guy she claimed was best friends with this woman, D-Block.

It looked like the two bodies around him were the guys who'd killed him. His wounds were consistent with what he knew of the Uzi, which was lying on the street as well. Jackson couldn't really put the story together yet.

But once crime scene investigators had gone over everything, then a specialist would begin putting together a play by play of what happened. Now he had to call Imani and let her know what happened.

***

"Nooo," Imani cried out.

The news messed her up. How much would she have to lose, she thought. It seemed to her as if D-Block was destroying her world. Ever since she had known this woman, her life seemed to be spinning out of control. No matter what she did, it seemed like Diane was coming out on top.

Imani made up her mind in that moment. She was through with Augusta, Ga. It was about time she moved back to Jacksonville, Fl. And let D-Block have Augusta.

***

Juanita was already putting the next stage of her own plan into action. She'd already spoken with Diane about it. Since she'd moved so many Hispanics to Augusta, they were needing more room to branch out. Since Diane knew they would be buying their product from her, she wouldn't have to worry about any funny business. The relationship that the two of them held was bonded by respect, especially since Juanita and Justice had become a serious Boo thang.

"Pedro, I think it'll be good if you moved your kings into Harrisburg," she told the Puerto Rican that sat on the hood of his old school box Chevy, smoking a blunt and drinking a beer.

"How much control are we going to have?" he asked.

"We don't want to aggravate the situation. That wouldn't be a good idea," she explained.

The point wasn't to start a race war, nor to cause the police to bring in immigration because eighty percent of them were illegals and could be deported.

"You go in and do it the right way," she said. "And you won't have any problems. There will still be some blacks in the area. And some of them will hustle. That ain't an issue. Just don't start nothing that draws unnecessary attention."

Considering how they'd moved on Central Ave thus far, Juanita couldn't see it being that hard. The blacks didn't have a problem with them as long as there was peace between the gangs. Juanita knew that their main issue would be between themselves, which was why she was separating the Puerto Ricans from the Mexicans. The two were alright for the most part. But, left alone for too long, and there would be a problem between them.

"Si," was all Marco said.

Juanita's word was pretty much law. She was, after all, the Hispanic Queenpin. And she was more than fair with everybody. No one group would make more money than the other, unless they personally fucked up their packages.

Once she was sure everyone understood the new rules, she went into one of the houses and spoke with the older Mexican woman inside. She was like a great-grandmother to the neighborhood, so she had to pay her respects.

***

Halfway to Atlanta, Diane began to realize where they were headed. She didn't know where exactly in Atlanta they would end up, nor did she know why, other than they were trying to escape their punishment.

"So, wat im do after dis work done?" Alicia asked.

"You mean what are we going to do?" Diane asked.

Then she thought about it. Juanita would be putting her people into position. With that being done, she would have far more power in Augusta. There wouldn't be too many people who would dare try her.

"I'm not sure really. I do know that I'm getting too old to be out here running the streets," Diane said.

"Well, yu can retire and mi could run de business. Mi be a good boss," Alicia threw at her.

Amazingly, Diane glanced at her sideways as she considered it. But then there were other factors to think about. What would Big Dredd think about his niece being put into a position like that?

"Nah, love. You ain't ready yet. You barely know Augusta like that. And Big Dredd wouldn't want you in harm's way like that," Diane explained.

Alicia thought about that as she drove. She really wasn't sure if she wanted to be a boss or not. It was really a joke when she said it, but Diane had actually thought about it.

"It looks like they're going to the airport," Diane said.

Alicia jumped off the 285 and continued following the Range Rover. Off in the distance, she could see the airplanes coming and going.

"We're going to have to hit them before they enter the terminal. We won't be able to go farther than the parking lot with our guns," Diane explained.

She then pulled her nickel plated Desert Eagle out and checked the clip. She hadn't used it at all tonight, yet. But her goal had been to kill this pretty boy muthafucka, Don Angelino, because he'd just shown her a lack of respect. In her mind, Diane felt like she'd been fair with him.

"Get closer. We ain't gon' get but one shot at this, so we've got to make it count," Diane said.

Alicia closed the distance between them and the Range Rover. They were just now entering the extremely large parking lot of the airport. It was now or never.

Chapter Twenty-One

Teflon read the message on his phone.

"The plane landed ten minutes ago. But it'll be another ten minutes before it's ready to take off again."

"But won't it take longer than that to get through the terminal?" Black Money asked.

He'd never flown to or from New York with them before, so he didn't fully understand how it went.

"Not really, bruh," Teflon said. "We'll be going to the private boarding gate, not public passenger boarding. We've done it before," he explained.

Black Money bobbed his head up and down. He whipped the Range Rover through the parking lot until he found a good long-term parking space.

"Alright, nephew, grab your bag and head for the front. We'll be right behind you," Teflon said.

But just as they were all exiting the truck, there was a tire screech. They turned and looked, then saw the Nissan Armada speeding towards them.

"Run, nephew," Teflon called out just as the SUV turned and slid sideways.

Both Diane and Alicia exited the Armada with their guns out. Luckily, Black Money hadn't stashed his M-P 5k yet. He reached back into the Range Rover and grabbed it off the seat. When he turned, Black Money squeezed the trigger.

***

Diane dived and landed on the side of another car. She lost complete sight of Alicia. But she did catch a glimpse of Don Angelino as he raced towards the airport entrance. However, there was nothing she could do to stop him. From behind the car, she returned fire, forcing Black Money to duck behind the Range Rover.

She paused a moment and looked around the parking lot. Diane was looking for a way to get closer to where the shooter was. While crouched down, she moved around cars, trying to get closer to where Black Money was.

***

Alicia went after Angelino, weaving in between cars. But she lost physical sight of him pretty fast. She just knew that he was running in this direction, so she continued, with her Glock 9mm out, ready to shoot. She lifted her head when she thought she saw movement again. And just as she did, the window of a Lexus 570 shattered. When she looked in the other direction, she saw Teflon duck behind a minivan.

"Blood clot," she stressed.

Then she changed the direction she'd been running in. There was no need chasing Angelino with this nigga after her.

***

He wasn't exactly scared. Don Angelino continued moving carefully between the parked cars. He could hear the gunfire behind him.

Once again, he cursed himself because he didn't make a better decision when dealing with D-Block. When he looked up, he could see the doorway to the Airport entrance clearly. He was almost there. Angelino picked up his pace and pushed just a bit harder. When he was able to reach out and grasp the door handle, he sighed with relief. He pulled it open and stepped inside.

Angelino maneuvered his way through the few people who must've been waiting for late flights. When he reached the desk, he asked the woman behind it about the private Lear jet.

"Yes, sir. The Lear is waiting for you, sir," the woman behind the counter told him.

Angelino followed behind the attendant the woman pointed out to show him the way.

***

"Fuck," Black Money cursed as his clip ran empty.

He knew that there was another full clip inside of the truck. But he couldn't take the chance trying to get to it. He didn't know how many clips the bitch shooting at him had. The more he thought about it, though, it didn't really matter. If he didn't go for the extra clip and this bitch caught him down bad, he'd be going out bad. If he made a move for it, his chances were closer to 50/50 that he would come out on top. Black Money had always been a gambling man, so he decided to take a chance.

He grabbed the handle of the door, pushed the button, and heard the lock release. Then he paused a moment, listening for footsteps. When he was sure he didn't hear any movement, he pulled the door open and peeked up inside. The extra clip was lying between the seat and the center console. All he had to do was lean in and reach.

But just as his fingertips touched the clip, "Kha Chink."

Black Money heard the sound of the gun being cocked, sending a round into the chamber. His body froze. A second later, he felt the barrel of the gun being pressed to the back of his head.

"Wait," he called out. "Let, let's make a deal."

He couldn't see who stood behind him. But after another second, he swallowed. Black Money knew they were thinking about it.

"Don, I mean Angelino, didn't grab all of the money when he ran." He swallowed. "There, there's about a quarter million in the bag inside," he said. "And you think I need ya to find it?" D-Block said. Then she squeezed the trigger.

***

Alicia heard the shots and assumed that, either Diane was dead, or the nigga she'd been after. She could hear the police sirens getting closer by the second. It seemed to be taking her forever to find this nigga. But as she rounded the last corner, she saw him turn.

Boom.

"Aah," she screamed as the slug tore into her left arm and spun her halfway around.

"Boom. Boom. Boom.

Three more shots followed. But each of these slugs dug into the wall of the building she stood next to, sending brick chips into the air with dust.

Alicia clutched her arm with the gun still in her right hand.

"Jah save di natty dread. Don let dis downpressor kill me," she chanted.

Then she took a few deep breaths and looked around. She could see where the nigga hid behind a sign that had the name of the airport on it. Alicia clenched her teeth and slipped backwards into the shadows. She made her way quietly around the other side.

Teflon ejected the clip that was spent and dug into his back to pull out the extra one he had in his waistband. He knew he'd hit the bitch. He just didn't know how bad it was. More than likely, she was on the run now. He had to catch up to Angelino so that the plane could take off. He wasn't sure how long his nephew could convince the pilot to wait.

He took a quick peep around the sign, and didn't see the crazy, dreadlock-wearing bitch. Teflon waited a ten count. Then he put one foot in front of the other and gave himself a burst of energy to run.

"Boo yaw, blood clot pussy boi. Ear."

Boca. Boca. Boca.

Alicia didn't even care that she was unloading her clip into the niggaz back. She was so pissed about being shot that it didn't even matter to her. She didn't ease up on the trigger until Teflon's body went down, shaking on the ground.

"Dem arm-stick banggarang, Boo-Yaka, dem go rass." Alicia was in the process of talking to herself as she walked back towards where she had left Diane.

***

"Come on, Unc," Angelino said to himself as he sat in the window side seat, looking out.

In one hand, he held a glass of Hennessy Paradis on the rocks. He'd made the drink as soon as he got on the private Lear jet. The bar was stocked with several cognacs and even some champagnes. Angelino needed something to calm his nerves. He hadn't thought that he would even make it to the plane, much less get away, especially when they realized this crazy bitch had followed them all the way to Atlanta.

Whatever he had done to warrant this type of bad energy, Angelino told himself that he needed to change it. He was going to have to start over anyway. It was over with for Augusta, even if he came back in six months, or a year. These muthafuckaz had killed his whole crew. There would be no one left.

"Excuse me, sir," the co-pilot said as he entered the area of the plane where Angelino sat.

At first, he thought that it was kind of unusual. The Italians weren't known for employing blacks over whites. Some of them couldn't care less what kind of skills a black person had, they'd be the last one to get a job. And here it was, he found himself looking up into the face of a bald head, older black man, with a neatly trimmed goatee. The man wore the co-pilot uniform without the hat. He smiled when he spoke, very professional.

"Yes, what is it?" Angelino asked.

The man came to stand only five feet away from him. He looked like he had something important to say.

"I was asked to give you a message before," the co-pilot said.

"Before what?" Angelino asked, vexed.

Then his eyes grew wider as he watched the other man pull out the gun. The killer held a black Beretta M9, special edition. It used 9 mm para bellum ammunition. There were fifteen rounds in the magazine, and a military dot upon the sight. The gun also carried a laser sight attached to the bottom of its barrel, which also stopped it from kicking upward. This gave the gun a thirteen percent increase in weight. Attached to the very end of the barrel was a titanium four-inch extension sound suppressor, with air holes drilled into it.

Once he was sure of all that. The killer checked the bags. He found the one with the money and left the plane. There was nothing else for him to do.

***

Diane managed to get Alicia to the doctor they had on standby. She'd had to park the Armada three blocks away and walk her the rest of the way. Then it took the doctor nearly an hour to get the bullet out of her shoulder and sew her back up. But she was going to live to see better days.

What hurt Diane the most was the text she received informing her that Maine hadn't made it. With all of the history between them, that was really hard for her. But she told her self that she'd do right by his kid. That, she promised herself, even though she was going to hate dealing with his baby's mother, Imani.

The second text from Juanita. On her end, things were good. She'd divided up both areas with her people. All they were awaiting on were their marching orders.

The only thing that bothered her was that this nigga Don Angelino had gotten away. She suspected that he'd come back, and be an even bigger problem, until she received the text from Young Castro. Diane had to re-read it several times before she understood what it was. Then a photo came through. A snapshot of Angelino slumped dead on the plane. She went back and re-read the message again.

"I told you I've got you, ma. I made you the Queen of Augusta for a reason. And anyone who contests, disputes, or challenges your throne, gone pay for it with their lives. This is Thug Life, ma. Thug Life," the text read.

But without the photo, it didn't add up. Now the other pieces began to fall into place. The whole time she assumed Damian and Justice were out killing people, it really wasn't them. It was Young Castro, but she would have never suspected him of it.

Trai'Quan

Chapter Twenty-Two

"What? Nah, nah. The numbers ain't right. Re-do 'em and then send them back to me."

Big Swole was talking on his phone as he left the courthouse. This one court appearance had been hanging over his head for quite some time now. If the state hadn't pushed the issue, the Feds would have let it continue growing into a RICO case. And no nigga wanted to find himself faced with something like that.

He made his way down the steps of the courthouse and out to the large carport parking across the street. This was the one time that he made any moves without a whole team of his dogs with him. When he reached his Lexus GS, he wasn't thinking about anything other than the fact that he'd just beat a case in court. So when he unlocked the car and slid inside, the last thing he expected was to feel the barrel of a gun placed to the back of his neck.

"Don't do nothing stupid. I just want to talk to you, and deliver a message," the voice said.

Big Swole visually relaxed. He tried to look up into the rearview to get a look at the man. But the mirror had been turned.

"Listen, bruh, I'm a million dollar nigga," Big Swole boasted. "I can pay you whatever. All you gotta do is let me know who pulling the strings. Crip, G.D., another Blood set, who?"

"I was told you were smarter than that," the voice spoke from behind him. "You assume this is some local gang banging shit. Well it ain't. So shut up and listen to what I tell you."

Big Swole's head bobbed and his heartbeat picked up once again.

"Whatever beef you had down in Augusta, you need to dead that. Any ill thoughts you got against the Street Queen, you need to dead that. There are some real powerful people behind her. And it ain't about yo millions. If these people send me back to New York about you," he paused for effect. "Nobody will be able to save you. And all of your bros will watch their big homie die in agony," the voice declared.

Big Swole sat there and swallowed the lump in his throat. He'd been threatened before, everyone had at one point in time. But it was this threat that made him a believer.

"So, are we good?" the voice asked.

"Yeah. Yeah, we're good," Big Swole said.

No sooner had he said it did darkness enfold him. The man in the back seat hit him over the head with a blackjack. Then he exited the car and calmly walked back to his own car.

***

"Yo. Yo, who is it, Pah?" Young Castro asked as he answered the knock to his office door. He was in the middle of doing some paperwork.

He stopped and looked up when his assistant manager stuck his head inside. "Uh. She's here," the white guy said.

Young Castro held his hand up and waved for him to show her in. He'd thought to see her two days ago, but she hadn't shown up. He looked up now as D-Block stepped into the office.

"The Street Queen. What's up, baby?" he asked with a smile on his face.

Diane stood there looking like Michelle Obama in her Roberto Cavalli dress and Giuseppe heels.

"Mnnhm. Whatever, nigga. Where your shadow at?" she asked as she took a seat in the chair across from the desk, and crossed her leg.

"Who, Jeeta? Pah out somewhere taking care of business." He continued to smile.

"You sure he ain't out there killing people?" she said.

"What? Who, Jeeta? Nah, Pah be about the business. I have other people who do that stuff. Besides, I know you ain't complaining," he said.

"No." She nodded out of respect.

"Listen, ma," Young Castro began. "Let me be straight up with you. Right now, your services are very valuable. And I appreciate you. So if some fool comes along and disrespects you, he disrespects me. And we can't have that, ma. Besides, I've got an upcoming project I think I'll need you to oversee. So I need you to have a clear head about it," he explained.

Diane arched her right eye brow at that. "And what exactly do you got your crooked hands in this time?" she asked.

"Now see, ma, I wouldn't exactly call a nigga crooked. I've never done bad business," he laughed.

She rolled her eyes. "That's not what I meant, nigga," Diane stated.

"I know, I know. So here's the thing. I have two areas I need a foothold in. The first is Charleston, SC. And I don't have the time to go down there and find a point man," Young Castro explained. "And the second one is Savannah, Ga. But I've heard they got a crazy nigga down there, some Jamaican nigga calling himself Rude Face. I'm still debating that, though."

Since his intel on the Rude Face nigga had come from another source, he was still waiting to see if he got the green light on it. But if he did have to send her down there, he was thinking it might be best to send Damian, Justice, and Thugg down there first. Let them run through the C-Port and put shit into perspective before the Street Queen showed up.

***

"Yeah, yeah, I hear you, family," Noel said as the person on the other end of the phone spoke.

"Ok, well here's the thing. If I green light this operation, my people may have to come through hard at first. That nigga, Ocean, he's gon' have to go first. We'll deal with the rest of them," he explained.

Ocean was the name of a big drug kingpin in Savannah. He was plugged in with some Mexican Zetas that had a big thing down in Miami. Ocean was the real power behind Rude Face.

"Okay, ok, fam. Let me send a message to these people and see what's good."

Noel ended the call, and then sent a quick text to Young Castro. When Carnilito first hit him and said that he was having some problems in Savannah, Noel told him he really didn't have anyone down there. But as he listened to the situation with this guy, Ocean. He came to the realization that this could be a play for D-Block.

He looked at the text that came back. Then he smiled.

Noel pulled up Francis' number and sent him a text, too. After killing Angelino and the Bloods that were bothering Diane, he'd also asked Francis to visit this guy, Big Swole, because they needed to make sure that the message was clear.

After that text, he sent one more before he put his phone up for the night. So far, everything seemed to be coming together, especially if this last thing came out right. That would really make a lot of shit easier. Noel sighed. Then he turned his phone off. Well, tomorrow wasn't far away…

***

"Wait a minute. You want me to do what?"

Francis looked across the table at the other man. He wasn't about to re-explain it. He knew that he'd made himself clear from the start.

"Listen, the money's in the bag. You can either take it, or leave it. The choice is yours. But know this," Francis said. "You'll make more with us, than against us."

Francis didn't even look around as he stood up. He turned and left the sports bar.

GBI Agent Jackson Anthony reached down and pulled the bag closer to his feet. He still couldn't believe what just happened. He glanced around the sports bar as he sipped his beer. Then his mind thought it over.

He was being given two hundred fifty thousand dollars just to overlook this woman's business. He swallowed the lump in his throat. This Diane Blaylock woman seemed to be more powerful than he'd thought. The man he'd just gotten the money from had known everything about him, even the illegal things that nobody else knew. He didn't see how that was possible. And it was all because of the Street Queen.

To Be Continued...
Thug Life 4
Coming Soon

Submission Guideline

Submit the first three chapters of your completed manuscript to ldpsubmissions@gmail.com, subject line: Your book's title. The manuscript must be in a .doc file and sent as an attachment. Document should be in Times New Roman, double spaced and in size 12 font. Also, provide your synopsis and full contact information. If sending multiple submissions, they must each be in a separate email.

Have a story but no way to send it electronically? You can still submit to LDP/Ca$h Presents. Send in the first three chapters, written or typed, of your completed manuscript to:

LDP: Submissions Dept
Po Box 944
Stockbridge, Ga 30281

DO NOT send original manuscript. Must be a duplicate.

Provide your synopsis and a cover letter containing your full contact information.

Thanks for considering LDP and Ca$h Presents.

<u>Coming Soon from Lock Down Publications/Ca$h Presents</u>

BOW DOWN TO MY GANGSTA

By **Ca$h**

TORN BETWEEN TWO

By **Coffee**

THE STREETS STAINED MY SOUL **II**

By **Marcellus Allen**

BLOOD OF A BOSS **VI**

SHADOWS OF THE GAME II

TRAP BASTARD II

By **Askari**

LOYAL TO THE GAME **IV**

By **T.J. & Jelissa**

IF LOVING YOU IS WRONG... **III**

By **Jelissa**

TRUE SAVAGE **VIII**

MIDNIGHT CARTEL IV

DOPE BOY MAGIC IV

CITY OF KINGZ III

By **Chris Green**

BLAST FOR ME **III**

A SAVAGE DOPEBOY III

CUTTHROAT MAFIA III

DUFFLE BAG CARTEL VI

HEARTLESS GOON VI

By **Ghost**

A HUSTLER'S DECEIT III

KILL ZONE **II**

BAE BELONGS TO ME III

A DOPE BOY'S QUEEN III

By **Aryanna**

COKE KINGS V

KING OF THE TRAP II

By **T.J. Edwards**

GORILLAZ IN THE BAY V

3X KRAZY III

De'Kari

THE STREETS ARE CALLING II

Duquie Wilson

KINGPIN KILLAZ IV

STREET KINGS III

PAID IN BLOOD III

CARTEL KILLAZ IV

DOPE GODS III

Hood Rich

SINS OF A HUSTLA II

ASAD

KINGZ OF THE GAME VI

Playa Ray

SLAUGHTER GANG IV

RUTHLESS HEART IV

By Willie Slaughter

FUK SHYT II

By Blakk Diamond

TRAP QUEEN

By Troublesome

YAYO V

GHOST MOB II

Stilloan Robinson

KINGPIN DREAMS III

By Paper Boi Rari

CREAM II

By Yolanda Moore

SON OF A DOPE FIEND III

By Renta

FOREVER GANGSTA II

GLOCKS ON SATIN SHEETS III

By Adrian Dulan

LOYALTY AIN'T PROMISED III

By Keith Williams

THE PRICE YOU PAY FOR LOVE III

By Destiny Skai

I'M NOTHING WITHOUT HIS LOVE II

SINS OF A THUG II

By Monet Dragun

LIFE OF A SAVAGE IV

MURDA SEASON IV

GANGLAND CARTEL IV

CHI'RAQ GANGSTAS IV

KILLERS ON ELM STREET II

JACK BOYZ N DA BRONX II

By **Romell Tukes**

QUIET MONEY IV

EXTENDED CLIP III

THUG LIFE III

By **Trai'Quan**

THE STREETS MADE ME III

By **Larry D. Wright**

IF YOU CROSS ME ONCE II

ANGEL III

By **Anthony Fields**

FRIEND OR FOE III

By **Mimi**

SAVAGE STORMS III

By **Meesha**

BLOOD ON THE MONEY III

By J-Blunt

THE STREETS WILL NEVER CLOSE II

By K'ajji

NIGHTMARES OF A HUSTLA III

By King Dream

IN THE ARM OF HIS BOSS

By Jamila

MONEY, MURDER & MEMORIES III

Malik D. Rice

CONCRETE KILLAZ II

By Kingpen

HARD AND RUTHLESS II

By Von Wiley Hall

LEVELS TO THIS SHYT II

By Ah'Million

MOB TIES II

By SayNoMore

BODYMORE MURDERLAND II

By Delmont Player

THE LAST OF THE OGS II

Tranay Adams

FOR THE LOVE OF A BOSS II

By C. D. Blue

Available Now

RESTRAINING ORDER **I & II**

By **CA$H & Coffee**

LOVE KNOWS NO BOUNDARIES **I II & III**

By **Coffee**

RAISED AS A GOON I, II, III & IV

BRED BY THE SLUMS I, II, III

BLAST FOR ME I & II

ROTTEN TO THE CORE I II III

A BRONX TALE I, II, III

DUFFLE BAG CARTEL I II III IV V

HEARTLESS GOON I II III IV V

A SAVAGE DOPEBOY I II

DRUG LORDS I II III

CUTTHROAT MAFIA I II

By **Ghost**

LAY IT DOWN **I & II**

LAST OF A DYING BREED I II

BLOOD STAINS OF A SHOTTA I & II III

By **Jamaica**

LOYAL TO THE GAME I II III

LIFE OF SIN I, II III

By **TJ & Jelissa**

BLOODY COMMAS I & II

SKI MASK CARTEL I II & III

KING OF NEW YORK I II,III IV V

RISE TO POWER I II III

COKE KINGS I II III IV

BORN HEARTLESS I II III IV

KING OF THE TRAP

By **T.J. Edwards**

IF LOVING HIM IS WRONG…I & II

LOVE ME EVEN WHEN IT HURTS I II III

By **Jelissa**

WHEN THE STREETS CLAP BACK I & II III

THE HEART OF A SAVAGE I II III

By **Jibril Williams**

A DISTINGUISHED THUG STOLE MY HEART I II & III

LOVE SHOULDN'T HURT I II III IV

RENEGADE BOYS I II III IV

PAID IN KARMA I II III

SAVAGE STORMS I II

By **Meesha**

A GANGSTER'S CODE I &, II III

A GANGSTER'S SYN I II III

THE SAVAGE LIFE I II III

CHAINED TO THE STREETS I II III

BLOOD ON THE MONEY I II

By J-Blunt

PUSH IT TO THE LIMIT

By **Bre' Hayes**

BLOOD OF A BOSS **I, II, III, IV, V**

SHADOWS OF THE GAME

TRAP BASTARD

By **Askari**

THE STREETS BLEED MURDER **I, II & III**

THE HEART OF A GANGSTA I II& III

By **Jerry Jackson**

CUM FOR ME I II III IV V VI

An **LDP Erotica Collaboration**

BRIDE OF A HUSTLA **I II & II**

THE FETTI GIRLS **I, II& III**

CORRUPTED BY A GANGSTA I, II III, IV

BLINDED BY HIS LOVE

THE PRICE YOU PAY FOR LOVE I II

DOPE GIRL MAGIC I II III

By **Destiny Skai**

WHEN A GOOD GIRL GOES BAD

By **Adrienne**

THE COST OF LOYALTY I II III

By Kweli

A GANGSTER'S REVENGE **I II III & IV**

THE BOSS MAN'S DAUGHTERS I II III IV V

A SAVAGE LOVE **I & II**

BAE BELONGS TO ME I II

A HUSTLER'S DECEIT I, II, III

WHAT BAD BITCHES DO I, II, III

SOUL OF A MONSTER I II III

KILL ZONE

A DOPE BOY'S QUEEN I II

By **Aryanna**

A KINGPIN'S AMBITON

A KINGPIN'S AMBITION **II**

I MURDER FOR THE DOUGH

By **Ambitious**

TRUE SAVAGE I II III IV V VI VII

DOPE BOY MAGIC I, II, III

MIDNIGHT CARTEL I II III

CITY OF KINGZ I II

By **Chris Green**

A DOPEBOY'S PRAYER

By **Eddie "Wolf" Lee**

THE KING CARTEL **I, II & III**
By **Frank Gresham**
THESE NIGGAS AIN'T LOYAL **I, II & III**
By **Nikki Tee**
GANGSTA SHYT **I II &III**
By **CATO**
THE ULTIMATE BETRAYAL
By **Phoenix**
BOSS'N UP **I , II & III**
By **Royal Nicole**
I LOVE YOU TO DEATH
By Destiny J
I RIDE FOR MY HITTA
I STILL RIDE FOR MY HITTA
By **Misty Holt**
LOVE & CHASIN' PAPER
By **Qay Crockett**
TO DIE IN VAIN
SINS OF A HUSTLA
By **ASAD**
BROOKLYN HUSTLAZ
By **Boogsy Morina**
BROOKLYN ON LOCK I & II
By **Sonovia**
GANGSTA CITY
By **Teddy Duke**
A DRUG KING AND HIS DIAMOND I & II III

A DOPEMAN'S RICHES

HER MAN, MINE'S TOO I, II

CASH MONEY HO'S

THE WIFEY I USED TO BE I II

By Nicole Goosby

TRAPHOUSE KING **I II & III**

KINGPIN KILLAZ I II III

STREET KINGS I II

PAID IN BLOOD **I II**

CARTEL KILLAZ I II III

DOPE GODS I II

By **Hood Rich**

LIPSTICK KILLAH **I, II, III**

CRIME OF PASSION I II & III

FRIEND OR FOE I II

By **Mimi**

STEADY MOBBN' **I, II, III**

THE STREETS STAINED MY SOUL

By **Marcellus Allen**

WHO SHOT YA **I, II, III**

SON OF A DOPE FIEND I II

Renta

GORILLAZ IN THE BAY **I II III IV**

TEARS OF A GANGSTA I II

3X KRAZY I II

DE'KARI

TRIGGADALE I II III

Elijah R. Freeman

GOD BLESS THE TRAPPERS I, II, III

THESE SCANDALOUS STREETS I, II, III

FEAR MY GANGSTA I, II, III IV, V

THESE STREETS DON'T LOVE NOBODY I, II

BURY ME A G I, II, III, IV, V

A GANGSTA'S EMPIRE I, II, III, IV

THE DOPEMAN'S BODYGAURD I II

THE REALEST KILLAZ I II III

THE LAST OF THE OGS

Tranay Adams

THE STREETS ARE CALLING

Duquie Wilson

MARRIED TO A BOSS... I II III

By Destiny Skai & Chris Green

KINGZ OF THE GAME I II III IV V

Playa Ray

SLAUGHTER GANG I II III

RUTHLESS HEART I II III

By Willie Slaughter

FUK SHYT

By Blakk Diamond

DON'T F#CK WITH MY HEART I II

By Linnea

ADDICTED TO THE DRAMA I II III

IN THE ARM OF HIS BOSS II

By Jamila

YAYO I II III IV
A SHOOTER'S AMBITION I II
By S. Allen
TRAP GOD I II III
By Troublesome
FOREVER GANGSTA
GLOCKS ON SATIN SHEETS I II
By Adrian Dulan
TOE TAGZ I II III
LEVELS TO THIS SHYT
By Ah'Million
KINGPIN DREAMS I II
By Paper Boi Rari
CONFESSIONS OF A GANGSTA I II III
By Nicholas Lock
I'M NOTHING WITHOUT HIS LOVE
SINS OF A THUG
By Monet Dragun
CAUGHT UP IN THE LIFE I II III
By Robert Baptiste
NEW TO THE GAME I II III
MONEY, MURDER & MEMORIES I II
By **Malik D. Rice**
LIFE OF A SAVAGE I II III
A GANGSTA'S QUR'AN I II III
MURDA SEASON I II III
GANGLAND CARTEL I II III

CHI'RAQ GANGSTAS I II III

KILLERS ON ELM STREET

JACK BOYZ N DA BRONX

By **Romell Tukes**

LOYALTY AIN'T PROMISED I II

By **Keith Williams**

QUIET MONEY I II III

THUG LIFE I II III

EXTENDED CLIP I II

By **Trai'Quan**

THE STREETS MADE ME I II

By **Larry D. Wright**

THE ULTIMATE SACRIFICE I, II, III, IV, V, VI

KHADIFI

IF YOU CROSS ME ONCE

ANGEL I II

By **Anthony Fields**

THE LIFE OF A HOOD STAR

By **Ca$h & Rashia Wilson**

THE STREETS WILL NEVER CLOSE

By **K'ajji**

CREAM

By **Yolanda Moore**

NIGHTMARES OF A HUSTLA I II

By **King Dream**

CONCRETE KILLAZ

By **Kingpen**

HARD AND RUTHLESS
By Von Wiley Hall
GHOST MOB II
Stilloan Robinson
MOB TIES
By SayNoMore
BODYMORE MURDERLAND
By Delmont Player
FOR THE LOVE OF A BOSS
By C. D. Blue

BOOKS BY LDP'S CEO, CA$H

TRUST IN NO MAN

TRUST IN NO MAN 2

TRUST IN NO MAN 3

BONDED BY BLOOD

SHORTY GOT A THUG

THUGS CRY

THUGS CRY 2

THUGS CRY 3

TRUST NO BITCH

TRUST NO BITCH 2

TRUST NO BITCH 3

TIL MY CASKET DROPS

RESTRAINING ORDER

RESTRAINING ORDER 2

IN LOVE WITH A CONVICT

LIFE OF A HOOD STAR

Trai'Quan

CPSIA information can be obtained
at www.ICGtesting.com
Printed in the USA
LVHW010130300821
696398LV00008B/476